DARK BLUE

Dan Cohen

PAGE PUBLISHING
Conneaut Lake, PA

First originally published by Page Publishing 2022

ISBN 979-8-88654-558-6 (pbk)
ISBN 979-8-88654-559-3 (digital)

Printed in the United States of America

He unracked the Ithaca ten-gauge—what they call the Streetsweeper—and quietly opened the car door. Overhead, above the alley where he was parked, he could hear a man and a woman arguing in the unit on the top deck of the wooden tenement. The man stepped out onto the porch and stood in the shadows, reeling gently. He was hugely fat.

The man with the shotgun lifted it to his shoulder and steadied it. The fat man looked down and saw him. "Please. Put down your gun," said the man with the shotgun.

The fat man looked puzzled. An instant later, the look was gone, and so was the face, blasted into nothingness. The headless body pitched forward over the porch rail and fell into a snowbank.

There were sirens. The man with the shotgun began to move quickly. He bent down next to the body and plunged the dead man's hands deep into the snow.

He was walking back to his squad car when his backup arrived.

CHAPTER 1

Chief of police is not a civil service slot. You get to be chief because the mayor likes you.

You cease to be chief when he ceases to like you or when he ceases to be mayor. This happens frequently. In Sanasauk, there were six former chiefs of police serving in various capacities within the department, but mostly lining up their troops and plotting their returns to the seat of power. And there would soon be a seventh. There was about to be a new mayor. He had formerly been a congressman.

The United States Congress has several committees which take an ongoing interest in matters involving police work. It would be hard to find a committee which, if the members were so inclined, could be excluded from jurisdiction on police issues.

There's gun control, drug trafficking, labor racketeering, white-collar crime, hate crime, and organized crime. Unlike much of the mundane work of Congress, the public takes an interest in these matters, and they all are highly politicized.

For a long time, liberals in Congress were at a disadvantage when it came to getting high-ranking cops to take the liberal line in their congressional testimony. The riots of the sixties, the almost exclusively white male lower middle-class backgrounds that produced most cops, and the authoritarian, paramilitary structure of police departments, helped create an almost monolithically reactionary mindset among policemen.

Almost. But not exclusively.

William Timothy Reagan, blessed with the surname of the twentieth century's most conservative president, was a former Boston Police commissioner and a flaming liberal.

When the congressional liberals needed a high-profile cop to help balance the parade of law-and-order types, Reagan was at the top of the list. Not only would he testify in favor of *registering* handguns, he could make the liberals look moderate by pleading for legislation to *outlaw and confiscate* every pistol, revolver, automatic, semi-automatic, pepper pot, and derringer in the country not in the hands of an authorized law enforcement officer.

Reagan also knew how to play to the gallery.

"I walked a beat in Pigs Town."

Nobody knew quite where Pigs Town was, but it sounded awfully tough.

When Congressman Eric Sensaboe ("Vote Sensaboe for Sanasauk") decided to take his pension and retire from Congress after ten terms in order to run unopposed for mayor of Sanasauk, he asked Billy Reagan for some advice.

"In two months, I've got to appoint a chief. The whole damn Sanasauk Police Department is riddled with dissension and factions and one of America's leading collections of right-wing nuts. One of these clowns, a former chief, mind you, actually sits in a booth during the state fair and passes out nut cake brochures to anyone dumb enough to take one. You got a network. Do you know of anyone in that department who can handle the job?"

"No. And from what I hear, there isn't anyone. You gotta go outside the department."

"I don't think so, Billy. This is a weak-mayor, strong-council setup. I got one real responsibility: appoint a chief. I pass over the whole department and I got 1,200 cops mad at me."

"So? You appoint one of these guys, and you got him and twenty of his buddies kissing your ass and 1,180 cops mad at you. It's always us versus them, the ins versus the outs. Every department. Get a good man and he'll clean the place up and take the heat for you."

"I got that funny feeling I get sometimes. Is this the beginning of a pitch?"

"I wouldn't shit you. Of course it is."

"Who?"

"Deputy commissioner of police, Hartford PD, Harold J., not for Jesus, Fishman."

"A Jew."

"Yeah, that's what the J's for. Also a mensch."

"This is Sanasauk."

"Yeah, I know. He'll have to go a thousand miles to find a decent pastrami on rye, but so what? That's his problem. What you got going here is a guy who's tougher than hell, can handle all the Jew stuff they'll throw at him, and can't build a constituency of his own to use against you if you got to shake him."

"So what's the dark side? He's gotta have a history if he wants to make the jump."

"He fucked up during the riots. The chief was out of town playing hide the salami with his director of public relations, leaving Harold J. in charge, who, thanks to his laissez-faire approach to crowd control, every schvartz in Hartford now has a free twenty-one-inch color TV and a microwave."

"Jesus."

"Well, we all have our crosses to bear. That was three years ago, and he's been in the shithouse ever since. But like I say, he's a tough administrator, a good judge of people, absolutely fearless and honest, the press will love him, he's solid on every single police issue, and he'll be dead loyal to you. What the hell more can you ask for?"

Three days after he was inaugurated as mayor of Sanasauk, Eric Sensaboe sent the name of Harold Joseph Fishman to the Sanasauk City Council for confirmation as Chief of Police.

Billy Reagan had been right about a few things and wrong about a few things.

An hour after he was confirmed as chief of police, Fishman held his first press conference.

"The candy store is now closed," said Fishman. "For openers, contrary to what you may have seen on TV, police services are not dispensed out of precinct stations. We're going to shut down several precincts. Get more of our people out from behind their desks and out onto the street.

"People don't come to the precinct anymore to tell us about their lost kitty cats. They have phones. They call. We answer the phones. We go out and see them. The idea is that police go to the people so the people don't have to come to the police. Nothing gets redlined anymore.

"We're also going to massively increase our police presence by eliminating two-man squad cars. Again, two-man squads work great on TV 'cause you got all this dialogue and these relationship stories you can dream up. 'Hey, rookie, I don't never want to see you take your gun out and play with it while I'm driving one hundred miles an hour chasing this mad dog serial killer.' 'Hey, I've never had a female-gender-type person as a partner before. Shouldn't you really be home doing the diaper thing?'

"Why am I doing this? Because when you get police officers out on the street where the folks can see them, people are safer, and when they're safer, they can enjoy their lives and their neighborhoods more. And then there's the people who don't want to see us, the bad guys. The more they see of us, the unsafer they feel, and you have fewer bad guys doing fewer bad things.

"It all adds up to the same thing. The greater the police presence on the street, the better the response time, the lower the crime rate.

"Why hasn't this been done before? Because it could be some people saw this job as designed with the cops in mind. It's a lot easier to sit on your duff in a precinct house shuffling paper or in a squad car shooting the breeze with a partner than it is to be out there pulling an eight-hour shift all by your lonesome.

"I don't see my assignment as making life easy for cops. I see it designed with the public's protection in mind. And that's way I'm going to play it."

Billy Reagan was right. The press loved it.

He was wrong about the pastrami. The delights of the East Coast deli case were available not one hundred feet from Fishman's office.

And he was wrong about Fishman taking the heat off the mayor. Fishman's honeymoon—and the mayor's—lasted for six weeks, when the first cop killed in the line of duty in Sanasauk in thirteen years was shot to death on patrol in a one-man squad car.

At which point the shit came down bigtime.

"Chief, I assume you read the papers. You saw the Fed's ad? Fuzzy old two-bit camera picture of Grandpa Dave, grandson sitting on his lap? We killed a grandpa, Chief. That's what it says here."

"It could have happened in a two-man just as easy, Mr. Mayor."

"That isn't what it sounds like from the article—the front-page article—where it said that Officer David Hope, how's that for a name of a guy gets killed? Hope? 'According to the police version, Officer Hope parked his one-man squad car behind the stopped vehicle and approached the driver's side of the car from the rear, where he checked the license and registration of the driver. He then walked around in front'—in front—'of the stopped vehicle to check the identification of the passenger on the driver's side. As he was crossing in front of the car, the passenger on the driver's side reached out of the window and shot him.' How long had he been on the force?"

"Twenty-seven years. He was pulling the full load. In for the thirty."

"That's always the way. Why did I even ask. It's right here in the article. 'Officer Hope was three years from retirement.' All right, back to the basics. What did he do wrong besides walk in front of the shooter, when he can't even see the guy's hands?"

"Everything. He did everything wrong."

"Like what?"

"He didn't even wait for the check on the plates to come through. He was out there before he knew what he was dealing with. The car was stolen. There was no call for backup. I can get that out to the public."

"You mean leak that out, don't you? You're not going to publicly shit on the grave of a dead hero grandpa, are you?"

"The public has a right to know—"

"Oh, shit, Harold, don't give me that shit."

"Sir, with all due respect—"

"Chief, we're going to have an inspector's funeral for hero officer grandpa Dave Hope. You're going to be there, and I'm going to be there, and I'll make a few remarks and hand the widow the flag. The only thing you are going to say in public is that you're ordering a complete investigation, which should take about a month until this all quiets down, and that you're going to find the thugs that did this. Period."

"Yessir."

Three days after Dave Hope's funeral, the two occupants of the stolen car were killed after a long police chase that began on the outskirts of Sanasauk and ended as they fled across a muddy cornfield twenty miles outside town.

The police officers involved in the shoot-out were Sergeant John Steinmetz on patrol in a one-man squad, Officer Edward White on patrol in a one-man squad, and Officers Ramona Guiterrez and Samuel Witherspoon in a two-man squad.

The Internal Affairs investigation took two months and dealt with both the Hope killing and the cornfield shootings.

There was no mention of Dave Hope's failure to call for backup, but there was this:

> On February 14, one month and six days prior to the fatal shooting of Officer David Hope on March 22, the department instituted a revised policy regarding motorized patrols. SPD Regulation 4017-1099 called for the discontinuance of all uniformed two-officer motorized patrols, except with the signed approval of the watch commander, and the use of one officer motorized patrols for all uniformed personnel as standard operating procedure.
>
> In conjunction with SPD Reg. 4017-1099, on February 21, the Department issued SPD Reg. 4024-1099, which required all uniformed personnel to attend a mandatory departmental training course on the proper operation of one-of-

ficer motorized patrols. The training course consisted of a series of three one-hour seminars to be conducted by the precinct training officer over the two-week period following the issuance of SPD Reg. 4024-1099, commencing February 24 through March 10. The seminars included written materials, lectures, and a training film prepared by the department. Attendance was taken and recorded.

Our review of the attendance records and receipts for the written materials shows no evidence that Officer Hope attended any of these seminars or that he received the written materials. Further, there is compelling evidence that officers were not required to complete the course before being assigned to patrol duty in one-officer squad cars.

Our analysis of all attendance records (summaries attached as Appendix 3) discloses that 112 of the 356 personnel carrying out patrol duties during from February 14 through March 22, the date of the incident in which Officer Hope lost his life, had undertaken patrol duties in one-officer vehicles without having completed the training course.

At the time of his death, Officer Hope had served twenty-six years and seven months with the SPD, twenty-one years and one month on patrol duty, and five years and six months as a police liaison officer with the Sanasauk public school system.

Officer Hope operated a one-person departmental vehicle during his assignment as a police liaison officer. No special departmental training was required in the procedures and operation of a one-person vehicle for assignment as a police liaison officer.

During the twenty-one-year-and-one-month period Officer Hope served as a uniformed patrol officer, SPD policy authorized the operation of two-officer patrol cars, with the operation of one-officer patrol cars being reserved for emergency use or with the written approval of the watch commander.

In accordance with SPD Reg. 2878-0877 (attached as Appendix 4) regarding the preservation and destruction of official records, departmental records pertaining to the use of one-officer patrol cars exist only for the four years and three months preceding the death of Officer Hope (attached as Appendix 4) during which time Officer Hope served on motorized patrol. There is no record of Officer Hope having operated a one-person vehicle while serving on motorized patrol duty prior to February 14 of this year.

Based on the foregoing we conclude the following:

1) Officer David Hope did not receive training in the correct procedures and operation of a one-person patrol vehicle.

2) Officer David Hope's lack of training in the correct procedures and operation of a one-person patrol vehicle contributed to his death.

3) Officer David Hope's lack of training was caused by

   a) insufficient preparation and planning by superior officers for the change in departmental policy from two-person to one-person motorized patrols,

b) inadequate supervision by superior officers.

4) Appropriate disciplinary action should be taken in accordance with these findings.

On the shooting of the two suspects:

The attempted apprehension of the suspects Steven Hoover and Marvin Payne commenced at 0115 hours when Officer Edward White in a one-officer unit notified Civilian Dispatcher Rosemary Murphy that he had identified the suspect's vehicle traveling in an easterly direction on Highway 17, approximately .5 miles within the Sanasauk city limits and was in pursuit. Civilian Dispatcher Murphy notified all units in the area to join in the pursuit. Sergeant John Steinmetz in a one-officer unit and Officers Ramona Guiterrez and Samuel Witherspoon in a two-officer squad being driven by Officer Guiterrez joined in the pursuit.

A high-speed chase ensued with Officer White in close pursuit, and Sergeant Steinmetz and Officers Guiterrez and Witherspoon following and within visual contact throughout most of the pursuit. The suspects' vehicle spun out and left the road rounding a curve on Highway 17, approximately nineteen miles east of Sanasauk. The suspects abandoned the vehicle and fled on foot across a cornfield, the property of one Otis Mayfield, a farmer who resides in a private dwelling approximately eight hundred feet south of said cornfield.

Officer White pursued the suspects on foot at a distance of approximately ten yards. While in pursuit, Officer White identified himself as a police officer, commanded the suspects to halt or be shot, and fired two warning shots into the air. At a point approximately two hundred feet from the point at which the suspects abandoned their vehicle, the suspects turned to face Officer White, and having handguns in their possession, suspects Hoover and Ferris each fired upon the officer with said handguns, missing in each case. The rounds were not recovered. Examination of the handguns recovered from the suspects indicates each suspect fired one round.

Officer White returned fire. Ballistics determined that the round recovered from the body of suspect Hoover was fired from Officer White's handgun, a .357 Colt Trooper revolver. The round entered suspect Hoover's chest approximately in the center of his sternum and lodged in his spine at T 6, approximately eleven inches above his coccyx. The round that killed suspect Ferris entered his chest approximately two inches to the left of the center of his sternum and exited approximately at T 7 twelve inches above and one inch to the right of his coccyx. The round was recovered, and ballistics confirmed it was fired from Officer White's handgun.

Sergeant Steinmetz and Officers Guiterrez and Witherspoon arrived on the scene shortly after the exchange between Officer White and the two suspects. Sergeant Steinmetz and Officers White, Guiterrez, and Witherspoon were interviewed in connection with this report and were cooperative.

Based on the foregoing, we conclude
1) Officer Edward White, in fulfilment of his sworn duty to serve and protect and at the risk of his own life in the pursuit and the

attempted apprehension of suspects Steven Hoover and Marvin Payne, is to be commended for the distinguished performance of his duties in the best traditions of the Sanasauk Police Department;

2) Sergeant John Steinmetz, Officer Edward White, Officer Ramona Guiterrez, and Officer Samuel Witherspoon, in fulfillment of their sworn duty to serve and protect, acted with merit in the performance of their duties in the pursuit and the attempted apprehension of suspects Steven Hoover and Marvin Payne.

Respectfully submitted,
Captain David J. Howard
Supervisor
Internal Affairs

Lieutenant Walter M. Sprague
Assistant Supervisor
Internal Affairs

Omitted from the report was an inquiry into why Officers Guiterrez and Witherspoon were operating as a two-officer motorized patrol and happened to be cooped at an abandoned rock quarry a couple of blocks from where the car chase started, which could have been explained by reporting that just as the backup call came in, Officer Guiterrez was performing the ultimate act of intradepartmental and interracial harmony upon Officer Witherspoon.

The day after the mayor and chief got the Internal Affairs report, a copy was leaked to the press.

The mayor called the chief into his office.

"Chief, the city attorney reminded me that there's a provision in your employment contract that requires you to take a physical within a month of your confirmation. It's been a couple of months now. I think you better get on over to the Sanasauk Clinic and get it taken care of."

"Is it okay if I go to my own doctor?"

"No."

"Why not?"

"Because you've got a heart murmur."

"I've got a heart murmur?"

"Yeah, which will be detected during your routine examination."

"Yeah?"

"And cause you to announce your resignation for reasons of health. Billy will find you a spot, don't worry."

"Well, I'm not surprised."

"You could always force my hand, in which case, you will have taken your second fall in three and half years. I don't know if even a rabbi as good as Billy Reagan could help you out then. This way, all you got to do is go to your own doc. He'll see that we misread your EKG, give you a clean bill of health, and you're back in business. It's your call."

"We could have ridden it out."

"Yeah, maybe, but what the hell, it's always only a matter of time. Remember Billy Martin? Steinbrenner fired him and hired him five times. So one of the times he fires Martin, he hires Yogi. Yogi goes in the manager's office, looks in the drawer. There's two envelopes with his name on them. One of them says, 'Open this envelope first.' Inside, there's a note. Yogi reads the note. It says, 'The first time Steinbrenner gets pissed and threatens to fire you, call a press conference and blame me. Say, "It's all Martin's fault. Once I get my system working, things are going to get a lot better."'

"So Yogi does something Steinbrenner doesn't like, Steinbrenner threatens to fire him, and Yogi has a press conference and blames Martin, and things go along okay for a while until Steinbrenner gets pissed again. Yogi opens the second envelope. There's another note. It says, 'Prepare two envelopes.'"

"I didn't get two envelopes."

"No, you didn't. I'm sorry."

"I'm not so sure it ever would have really worked out here. The rabbi here, I mean the real rabbi in Sanasauk, called me and asked me to speak to the Men's Club. I go over there. The place is packed to the rafters. They had never even *seen* a Jewish cop before, much less a Jewish chief of police."

"You gave it your best shot. This damn Hope thing hadn't come down, you'd have been all right. You were doing good things too. Sometimes it's just better to be lucky than to be smart."

"So when's my doctor's appointment?"

"Tomorrow at 10:00 a.m. Please make the press conference for tomorrow afternoon."

CHAPTER 2

The thing about cops is they don't trust anybody, especially other cops. Starting the day they become cops, they begin the process of exclusion under the guise of cohesion.

When the mayor and the chief have finished their speeches and the graduation ceremony is over, the rookies arrange themselves into a reception line. There are relatives and wives and girlfriends and hugs and kisses and handshakes. For about two and half minutes, everybody loves everybody. Then two veteran cops start working the line, from opposite ends. One is with the Knights of Columbus, and the other is with the Masons. It doesn't matter what city you're in, except maybe New York, where there's a third guy, from B'nai B'rith; it's the same everywhere.

Catholics, Protestants, Jews. Most people think nobody bothers with that kind of stuff anymore? Bullshit.

"What's the Masons?" one guy asks.

"It's a non-Catholic organization," the recruiter says. He already knows who's what.

White versus Black versus Hispanic. Male versus female. Day watch versus swing shift versus dog watch. Uniform versus plain-clothes. Patrolman versus sergeant versus lieutenant versus captain versus inspector versus deputy versus chief. Homicide versus burglary versus robbery versus drugs versus gangs. And every badge versus internal affairs and the entire nonbadge world. It breaks down that way real fast. Who you are is who you aren't.

Why do they become cops? One guy says, "I wanted security. I took the exams for postman. I took the exams for fireman. Passed

14

everything. But the waiting list was like forever. Took the exams for cops. They needed cops. I'm a cop."

That's the majority report. Civil service mentality. No layoffs. Decent pension. Twenty and out.

Other guys want to help people. Other guys like the authority. Other guys like the action.

A young cop can go a couple of ways. He can become a thumper. Every department needs street cops who can handle anything and really like the rough stuff. The trouble is that cops like that rarely know where to draw the line. Even though the brass tries to cover for them, they always seem to be in the shit.

Eddie White sticks his baton hard into a protester's gut at an antiwar rally, and it costs the city $200,000. Nothing happens to Eddie, but that's just it. He could be a sergeant by now, but he's never going to make it.

John Steinmetz goes the other way. He sees all this and curbs his animal instincts.

There are times when he crosses the line. But never when anyone can see. It's the citizen's word against Steinmetz. And the citizen in question is invariably a very bad citizen.

So when there are complaints, and Internal Affairs and the front office and the Citizens Review Board consider them, what they get is what civil service is really good at giving them, lots and lots and lots of paper. The paper on Officer Steinmetz shows an officer with multi citations for service to the public above and beyond the call of duty. The scumbag's record shows a fuckup with an endless capacity for messing up his life and that of everyone around him.

Case closed. No one cares to believe the scumbag. Civil service has another feature that Steinmetz uses to his advantage: promotion by way of examination.

Most cops don't bother to crack the books because opportunities for advancement are few. Steinmetz doesn't wait until deaths and retirements open the list. He spends some of his time drinking it up with his buds and getting laid, but he spends more of it on the books.

When they finally post the openings, he's ready. He hasn't fouled up with any of the guys on the oral exam board either.

He gets the nod.

Sergeant John Steinmetz.

Stay on the freeway another fifty miles past the cornfield where Steinmetz and his fellow officers blew away two suspects, and you come to New Arnhem, where Steinmetz was born and grew up.

Steinmetz's grandfather left Germany with a new wife in 1888, the Year of the Three Emperors. He joined a couple of hundred other Rhinelanders in the fertile, rolling countryside of the New Arnhem River Valley, where he farmed and raised a family of four boys and three girls.

His sixth child, and third son, Joseph, left the farm for the city after having served as an infantryman in Pershing's First American Army and been bloodied in the second battle of the Marne.

The farm depression, which lasted from the end of the First World War until the Second, fell hard upon New Arnhem, where the economy depended upon farm income. Like Harry Truman, Joseph Steinmetz thought his war record would help attract customers to his dry goods business, and like Harry Truman, he was wrong. Unlike Harry Truman, he wound up as a guard/custodian in the New Arnhem Valley State Institute for the Feeble Minded.

After John was born, the third of three children and the only male, Marina Steinmetz told her husband that now that she had given him a son, enough was enough, and she moved into her own bedroom.

John liked athletics. He was good, but that was it, good. His best qualities as an athlete were nonathletic.

The fall, football season, was his weakest. He was neither very big nor very fast. He became the kicker, the one slot that, at the high school level, was the product of endless practice and determination.

Winter was his best season. He wrestled. In both his junior and senior years, he was the runner-up in the district 160-pound weight division. In the spring, he ran cross-country but didn't letter until his senior year.

By then, he had an idea of what he wanted to do. His one real talent had been art. From the time he was a high school freshman, he had done the illustrations for the school paper and the yearbook.

If there was a poster to be drawn for a school event, he designed it. When he was a senior, the feature columnist for the local paper wrote an article about John, which included John's rather unflattering caricature of the columnist. Unflattering or not, the columnist incorporated John's sketch into the masthead above his column.

There was no money for college, but the owner of the paper, who had originally suggested the column, had established a scholarship fund for worthy New Arnhemites. By no coincidence whatsoever, John received a full scholarship to the Payson Institute of the Arts in Sanasauk.

One year had been enough to convince him he did not have the ability to make a living as a commercial artist. During that year, he met a dancer, Emily Teague, in a life drawing class.

The first night she and John spent together she told him about the experience that had made her want to become a dancer. She had been taking lessons since she was four. Illana, the lady who ran the dance studio, was a Hungarian refugee who had danced professionally with her husband in the Ballet Magyar.

One Friday afternoon when Emily was a sophomore in high school, her mother got a call from Illana. She said the Ballet Magyar was in town, and she was going to perform her role as the lead in *Scheherazade* at the Saturday matinee. Andre, her husband, would reprise his role as the Slave. Illana asked Emily's mother if she would like to have Emily be in the ballet as a slave girl. She would be paid, like a real professional.

"Well, I'd never even seen a real ballet, but of course, I wanted to. When I got there, there were all the other girls from my class. We were standing in the wings and giggling like mad, and they gave us these tutus and these tiaras and these wand things and told us to put them on right there. Then the stage manager said, 'Okay, do you see her?' And there's this dancer who's actually with the company standing just off stage. 'You're going to enter right behind her. She'll be running, you run. When she stops, you stop. When she holds up her arms like this, you hold up your arms like this, and when she runs off stage, stage left, you run off stage after her.'

17

"Two seconds later, the dancer is running on stage, and we're running after her, doing this and this and this, and then we're running off stage. And the stage manager is waiting for us. He grabs the tiara and gives it to one assistant, grabs the wand and gives it to another assistant, hands us each a dollar and a half, and tells us to take off the tutus and get dressed and go out in front and watch the rest of the show. And our clothes are waiting there for us, just the way we left them a minute earlier, only now they're on the other side of the stage. I was hooked."

"Did you keep the dollar and a half?"

"Nope. Spent it. Hey, I was going to earn a couple million more. That's still the only show business pay I've ever gotten."

They lived together the last semester John was at Payson, but when the school year was over, and John told her he wouldn't be back, they broke up.

It was seven years before John had any contact with her again.

In addition to thumpers, there's another slot that has to be filled in every police department: fixer. This person is the unofficial representative of a certain union. The wheels of commerce would grind to a halt if professional movers and haulers were expected to obey every dumbass parking and traffic restriction the city dreams up. For a modern city to function, there has to be a not inconsiderable amount of double-parking, lane blocking, and meter violating.

Most cops understand this, but there are always a few hot dogs, rookies mostly, who regard a parking violation as an impeachable offense. For them, there is a cop, usually at the inspector level to indicate unquestionable authority, who straightens things out on these matters and other less benign offenses that require special attention.

Deputy Inspector Avery Arnold is the fixer on the Sanasauk PD. His list of Rent a Badges is one of the sources of his authority. Lots of cops want to pick up extra bucks off duty. Arnold rewards those who behave according to his set of rules with off duty work. The Police Federation, which is much like any other union except for the no-strike laws, also runs a business, Interim Security, providing off duty cops.

Avery Arnold and the Fed have reached an accommodation: Arnold provides off duty cops as bouncers for Sanasauk's bars; the Fed provides off duty cops as security for sports and entertainment events. Sanasauk, a middle-sized middle American, slightly but not too Eastern city, has a full menu of events and the usual complement of saloons for every market niche, so there's plenty of room for both Arnold and Interim Security.

Lots of cops work for both, but there's a slightly better odor to the Fed's operation. For one thing, Interim Security issues the paycheck, not some saloonkeeper, who may be operating in violation of the building code or letting dopers peddle coke in the back while a cop is checking IDs in the front. For another, saloons naturally tend to be rowdier than, say, a Billy Graham revival. However, on those rare occasions when things do get out of hand at an event, it tends to get really rowdy. Unlike a bar, where it's usually just one customer at a time in need of an attitude adjustment, when you've got a whole crowd of people going berserko, you've got a major problem.

Steinmetz regularly worked off duty in uniform for IS, but he only worked for Arnold in plainclothes. He was a birddog, checking whether the joints were operating within Arnold's relaxed interpretation of the law, and gauging the performance of the badges.

That's why Steinmetz walked into Buckets, a bar on River Square.

"John, I can't believe it."

"Yeah. Gee, you look great, Emmie."

"Thanks. What are doing here?"

"No, no, not what you think. I'm a little past the pickup scene. I'm lookin' for a guy works for us, see if he showed up here."

"Works for you? I thought you were a policeman."

"I am a policeman. I have a side business too. I work security for concerts and games, like the Steamers' games. Well, one of our guys, Eddie, got a little overzealous at one of the games, and we sent him to the minors for a while to get it back together. He's supposed to be working the door here checking ID, but I don't see him. I came down here to see if he showed up. What are you up to, Em?"

"Working as a paralegal and going law school nights at SU. I'll have it finished in two more semesters."

"Do you still dance?"

"Well, no. Unless you count dancing with my father at my sister's wedding last year. That kind of didn't work out."

"That can happen. I know."

"I've gotta tell you something, Johnny. You know that story I told you about the Ballet Magyar and all that."

"Ahh, yeah, I remember that. Great story."

"Well, it is a great story, but it happened to Goldie Hawn, not me. I read it in a Sunday supplement. I wanted to tell you that for such a long time, but I didn't know how. I basically got into dance because I didn't know what else to do with my life. But the lawyer thing is a little bit more realistic, more me. Doesn't hurt to be a good storyteller if you're a lawyer."

"That's what I hear."

She seemed as though she were about to cry. She was in a hurry to leave.

"Johnny, call me. I gotta go now. Call me, though. Please."

"I promise. I will, Em."

CHAPTER 3

There was a National Mayors Conference in Washington, but Eric Sensaboe didn't go. He didn't dare leave town without a permanent police chief in place.

He called Billy Reagan in Newton.

"I'm sorry it didn't work out, Mr. Mayor," said Reagan.

"It wasn't a good fit, Billy. Maybe we need a harp. You guys have a talent for telling folks what to do."

"Policemen, priests, and politicians. It's a gift. We tell 'em, they do the heavy lifting. If you ever want to see unvarnished hatred, watch a construction job with an Irish foreman and an Italian crew. They get the job done though."

"Billy, come out here. We need you."

"I'm not coming out there. Marilyn would kill me. You think Fishman was a fishman out of water? Who am I going talk to out there with nothing but squareheads and hunkies? Can't find a friendly face. I need that familiar visage. *Mein Landsmenn.*"

"Billy, you owe me one. You gave me a lame. I need someone who can talk to cops. Straighten this thing out here."

"I was a little surprised when Fish did that one-man squad thing. Doesn't mean anything. One-man squad, two-man squad. You need them both. You going to send a white cop into the ghetto in a one-man squad? That's a suicide mission. You going to have your coppettes do one-woman patrols? First one takes a round, you might as well swallow your own gun. You're never going to live it down. You going to send out rookies in one-man cars? I can't understand why he did that."

"I think he was trying to get on top of the job. Show he was in control."

"The thing you got to remember about street work is that it's an age thing. You need to put a few years under them before they can do it alone. Best years for a street cop are between twenty-five and thirty-five, few years either way. Too young, they're too quick-tempered. Too old, they're burnouts. That's why twenty and out is best for uniform guys. The first few years they're walking time bombs, and the last few years they're bombed out, period."

"Why in God's name did you send me that guy?"

"Well, I thought he could do it. I honestly did."

"What made you do it, Billy?"

"Remember when I told you about the riots. Where he covered up for his superior, out of town with his girlfriend?"

"Yeah."

"Well, that was Marilyn's kid brother. Fishman saved his bacon, took the heat. He's one tough Jew, but I guess he just doesn't understand how to manage people."

"Billy, what the hell do you do out there all day in Newton, anyway?"

"Actually, very little. My kids are both grown-up, living in California. I can't get my handicap under twenty, and I'm on every goddam interfaith committee there is and even some bullshit committee for Barney Frank? My old man would kill me. It's getting so I can't decide whether to order corned beef and cabbage or corned beef on rye."

"Two years. A sabbatical, kind of. You've never had your own department."

"Yeah, Boston, my father was a meter reader for the gas company. There's five hundred third generation on the job harps ahead of me."

"Eighty thousand. I can get it for the right guy."

"You got some problems out there. The Fed is a bigger influence on police policy than you are or the newspapers or any of the council. Whoever runs that department has got to take down the police union. That is not a popular move for a Democratic administration, but either they run the force or the chief runs it. When push comes to shove, who are you going to back? That's the question, not one-man cars or residency or moonlighting. It's who runs the show."

"I can't let the Fed run this department. I can't get ahold of this thing as mayor unless I have a chief who can take hold. You. You can do it. I will back you one hundred percent. But you cannot blindside me again. I need your loyalty."

"If I were to do this, you would have my one hundred percent loyalty. But there are conditions. You will have to stay out of the kitchen. I run the department. You'll announce policy 'cause you're the guy who runs for office, but I'll be the guy who's going to whisper it in your ear first. Remember that lady mayor of San Francisco? Senator now. God, is the name Fishman again."

"No, it's Feinstein."

"Okay, Feinstein. Night Stalker case. Serial killer. She has a press conference. Announces they have the ballistics on the murder weapon. Announces they have perfect impressions of the perp's shoe from two separate crime scenes. Cops standing there browning their drawers while she spills all this. Perp reads the paper, and the gun and the shoes go over the Golden Gate Bridge. No running amuck. No press conferences without clearing with me."

"I think we understand each other."

"Well, maybe. Like they say, the devil's in the details. I'll talk to Marilyn, but I don't think she'll go for it."

Three weeks later, Billy Reagan was sworn in as chief of the Sanasauk Police Department, his wife, Marilyn, at his side, in a ceremony in the anteroom outside the mayor's office. There was no formal press conference, but there were reporters present, and they had questions.

"Chief, what's your policy on one-man squads?"

"When appropriate, we're going to have one-officer squads. When appropriate, we're going to have two-officer squads. And if we have to, we'll figure out a way to pile more people into a squad car than the Barnum & Bailey."

"What do you think of Sanasauk?"

"A fine city which I've always admired because I've always admired Mayor Sensaboe."

"What are your goals?"

"To serve and protect."

"I mean what are your specific quantifiable goals? What would you consider a success in terms of reducing crime?"

"When there isn't any. My job is…A police officer's job is rewarding when you're helping people. It's frustrating though, because you're dealing with people who are not having their finest moments. A lot of them are angry or in a lot of pain or they're doing bad things. The public, the people who pay our salaries, they are our customers. We want to treat them with courtesy and respect the way anyone would treat their customers. We're going to be nice. We're going to be nice just as long as we can be nice, until we can't be nice anymore. And then we'll do whatever it takes to get the job done."

That was the sound-bite answer, and Reagan thought he had nailed it. It was time to get moving. He shook the mayor's hand again, bussed his wife on the cheek, and with a wave, walked out of the room down the hall to the chief's office.

The desk in his office was bare except for the family pictures he had put on it half an hour earlier. He pushed the buzzer next to the phone, and a middle-aged black woman in civilian clothes came in holding a stack of folders.

"Chief?"

"It's Celeste, isn't it?"

"Yes, sir."

"Okay, I can tell you're just dying to dump these on my lap. I bet you know exactly what I should do with each of them, don't you?"

"Oh, no, sir."

"Celeste, we're going to get along just fine so long as you don't shit me. C'mon, let's have some fun. You play Chief here. I bet you could run this office. I bet you have run this office for—how long you been here?"

"Nine years."

"Nine years, and I'm the fifth in that time, right?"

"Right."

"Okay, what's on top of your stack?"

They spent the rest of the afternoon together going through minor disciplinary matters, a property damage report from a raid on a crack house, a promotion list ("Hold off here. I'm not ready to approve this") and the overnight, a statistical summary of crimes reported in the last twenty-four hours with brief written summaries of the major incidents.

"No grievances from the Fed?"

"No."

"Any pending grievances? Leftovers?"

"Oh, yeah, but do you really want to see those today?"

"No. We done enough for one day, Celeste. You satisfied?"

"I think you know I am. You done this sort of thing before."

"Then let the word go forth."

"Now that ain't nice."

"Well, it does go forth, doesn't it?"

"Yes, but you aren't s'posed to notice."

"I notice."

"Are you going to notice everything?"

"Yep."

"My. My. We're in for an exciting time here."

"That we are, Celeste. That we are."

CHAPTER 4

"You stood me up," said Zeno Malkin.

"I did not stand you up," said Emily. "I told you, someone came in that I knew, and I thought you would prefer it if we weren't seen together."

Zeno Malkin was the son of a shoe salesman and a school nurse and spent the first forty-seven years of his life with his nose pressed up against the glass.

Zeno managed three years in community college before he decided he'd had enough and hooked on as a salesman with one of Sanasauk's lesser-stock brokerage firms. He was good at it, a quick study who earned a piece of the action by snaring a couple of dubious underwritings for his outfit.

One deal, Sanasauk Nation Exploration and Discovery, was typical of late bull market Initial Public Offerings that surface when novice investors, accustomed to making money on everything they touch, throw their last dollar into the market.

Our government is aware of the risks inherent in IPOs, but because we believe in a "free market," and because nothing can prevent a fool from being foolish, the "safeguards" that have been enacted to protect investors from the Zeno Malikins are laughably easy to circumvent.

One safeguard is the ritual known as the due diligence meeting. At a due diligence meeting, the brokerage house underwriting the securities invites the brokers from firms involved in the underwriting to eyeball the company's management, hear their pitch, and ask them questions. The brokers then are encouraged to indicate their commitments for as many shares as they think they can sell. In a bull market, a well-staged presentation can move practically any merchandise. Nothing in the law requires the due diligence meeting to be held in an atmosphere of austerity. Savvy brokers know that the stinkier the deal, the better the booze, the more lavish the spread. The best of the best to hype the worst of the worst. The Sanasauk Nation Dee was a blowout. It was the first time anyone could remember where the bar was open before, after and during the pitch. And the program did not get going until about two hours after the first bottle had been cracked. If the showroom of the Las Vegas Hilton had been the venue for the Sanasauk Nation deal, Zeno Malkin would have been the fin de siècle Elvis. He knew how to work the broker crowd.

The room had been set up in the usual fashion, with the bar in back and the speaker's podium in front of the rows of folding chairs. On each side of the podium was a large portable speaker, what you might see on the stage of the Las Vegas Hilton. There was another unusual feature: beside the podium was a table with a telephone on it.

The company's management, the tribal leaders, made a pitch which revealed no knowledge of the oil business and wound up with an invitation to visit the rez and enjoy a free buffet at the casino.

Then Zeno took over. His spiel had to do mostly with the enormous commission that attached to the sale of the shares, a sure sign the broker's only motive for laying off this bet on his customers was greed.

Just as he seemed about to wind it up, he looked at his watch and said, "It looks like it's time for the field report. We hooked up this phone to these speakers here so you can hear directly from our head geologist, Homer Pryme, who is, even as we speak, standing in the middle of the cow pasture that represents our key concession. This is a field so potentially huge, such an elephant, as they say in the trade, that I can only hint at the ocean of black gold, which it contains.

"Homer...Homer...come in please...are you there?" said Zeno, shouting into the phone.

A staticky voice barked back over the speakers.

"Yeah, I'm here."

"So what's going on? How does it look?"

"Don't look like nothing. We're drilling. Nothing's happening," said Homer. "Lemme go back to work."

There were a few snickers from the brokers.

"No, wait a minute, Homer," said Zeno. "Let's talk here a minute. Tell me about your geological formations and seismic studies and that sort of thing. Let the folks here know what's going on. How deep. What kind of drill bit…"

As Zeno drones on, a kind of deep growl begins to be heard on the speakers.

"Homer, can you hear me? We've got some kind of interference here."

The growl grows louder. Now it begins to sound like rainfall.

"Homer, come in please. I can't—"

"Shut up, you fool." It's Homer's voice over the din.

"What? What did you say?" Zeno is puzzled and indignant.

"I said, shut up, you idiot. Can't you hear it? Can't you hear it? GODDAMMIT, can't you hear it?"

The brokers have stopped snickering. The megawatt speakers have kicked in. Waves of sound pour off the stage. Mighty thud followed mighty thud. The sound became a roar, a tornado of noise.

"Homer, what is it?" says Zeno.

"What the hell do you think it is? It's oil. IT'S A GODDAMN FIVE-HUNDRED-FOOT TOWER OF OIL. OIL. OIL."

The line goes dead.

For a second or two, the room is dead quiet, not even the click of an ice cube.

Then, from the back of the room, a voice.

"I'll take ten thousand shares."

Then another.

"I'll take twenty thousand shares."

Another.

"I'll take one hundred thousand."

Pandemonium.

Sanasauk Nation Oil and Exploration never got above its original offering price. There was nothing to drill for on the Sanasauk reservation except what could be found in the pockets of the casino's customers. Homer, if that was his name, was standing a few yards from the casino parking lot, running a garden hose inside a garbage can while one of his confederates held a mike hooked up to a powerful amplifier, and another was banging the garbage can lid with a sledge hammer. Fortunately for Zeno and the other defendants in the inevitable lawsuits that resulted from the collapse of Sanasauk Nation, the plaintiff's claims foundered on the rocks of "sovereign immunity." This is a legal doctrine which holds that if anything bad happens on the rez, like falling on your ass while you're jumping up to yell "bingo," it's your tough luck, because it happened in another nation, not the US of A, so you aren't going to collect in our courts. Of course, you can always try it in theirs.

When Zeno was thirty-three, he married the unmarriageable daughter of an immigrant junk dealer who had made his fortune when the Korean War sent the price of scrap metal to the moon. The marriage gave him access to all the money he would ever need but not the status. He craved the acceptance of what passed for celebrities in Sanasauk, the blue bloods, the jocks, the showbiz types. Fawning, scheming, his only claims to entrée were his willingness to write a fat check for any charity or politician his betters were promoting and his role as an all-purpose dogsbody.

When a beard was needed, Zeno was the designated hitter. If a payoff had to be made to a greedy pol, Zeno was the bagman. In return, some of the beautiful people accepted Zeno and Sophie's invitations, and a few reciprocated by inviting the Malkins.

Zeno was no fool. He knew there would only be scraps unless he could acquire some panache. So he became an author. Or rather he hired a ghost, and the ghost became the author, and Zeno took the bows.

To everyone's surprise, including Zeno's, *Malkin Money*, a loosely knit collection of business homilies and self-help advice, became a best seller. It was what the trade called an airport book, something road warriors could read cover to cover in no more than two hours and find a couple of suck-in-your-gut and tough-it-out stories that could get them through the next hop. Two not quite as successful sequels were stamped out from the same mold, *Malkin the Falcon* and *Don't Downsize: Malkinize*, and then a syndicated column, "Malkin Talkin'."

The books generated profitable spinoffs: speeches, software, motivational films and tapes. These sideline businesses had the further advantage of allowing Zeno to keep all the proceeds, since the ghost's contract excluded him from any income from his work other than from the books. Zeno's stock brokerage business, which previously had been mostly a way for him to get out of the house in the morning, thrived in the wake of his celebrity. His career as a motivational speaker not only provided a means of escaping the redoubtable Sophie for the day, but for days, even weeks at a time. For those occasions, Zeno arranged to have company. Emily had known Zeno for about two years and taken a couple of short swings with him on the author circuit when he was promoting *Don't Downsize: Malkinize*. Apparently, it was so customary for authors to reward themselves for their labors by packing a sex toy on their promotional tours that the author jockeys who picked them up and wheeled them around for their interviews never bothered to ask her name, nor did Zeno bother to introduce her.

Recently, Zeno had become so brazen in his philandering that he began asking Emily out in Sanasauk.

"People around here know you're married, Zeno. I really don't think we should keep doing this," she said.

"So what. I don't care. I'm crazy about you."

"Zeno, this isn't just about you. It's about me too. I don't care to get the reputation of someone who goes out with married men. Think Monica, Zeno."

But Zeno would wear her down, and several times she consented to meet him in public. Buckets was her idea, a sports bar cum pickup parlor for the college crowd. It seemed unlikely they would be seen together by someone she knew.

"You're my administrative assistant. What's the matter with being seen having a drink with your administrative assistant?"

"I'm not your administrative assistant. I'm a paralegal. I work for your lawyer."

"Okay, so why didn't you wait? You could've just said we were having a legal conference."

"Zeno, this guy's a cop. I used to go with him. I know cops. They're suspicious. It's their nature."

"Are you seeing him?"

"This is someone I haven't seen in seven years."

"I don't like it. I don't like what you did to me."

"Jesus, Zeno, for a world-class expert, you're a world-class expert on making something out of nothing."

"All right. You really can't blame me. I want so much to see you, and when we make a date and you don't show up, it hurts me. Perhaps I have overreacted. I apologize."

"Zeno…Zeno, I don't think I can go on with this anymore. It just isn't right. I see this person I used to know, and I'm afraid he's going to see you, and my heart just sinks. I feel so… It just makes me feel so cheap. So damn cheap. I'm sorry, Zeno."

"Wait a minute. This is getting out of hand. This is going too far."

"No. I should have said this before. It's hard for me to say what I feel sometimes. I've felt this way a long time. Even on the trips. You have been very good to me, Zeno, but this is not working for me anymore. I can't do it. I can't see you anymore. I'm sorry. I'm very sorry."

And she hung up.

It wasn't just losing her mind bet with herself about being seen by someone she knew at Buckets. It was seeing John that did it.

She didn't really think he would call. She knew she had sounded desperate. Just when she had almost gathered enough courage to call him, there he was, not just on the phone, but standing there, outside the door of her apartment, ringing the bell, with a stupid bunch of flowers in his hand.

"Mommy, Mommy, there's someone at the door," said Katie.

"Who's there? Do we know him?"

"It's a man, Mommy. He has something in his hand."

"Oh god, what's this about?" said Emmy. And then she saw that it was John and his flowers.

"Oh John, John. My god, it's you. Come in. Come in here. Oh god, John. John, this is Katie. My daughter, Katie. Katie, this is John. He's an old friend, dear. He's come to see us. Look, he's brought us some flowers. Isn't that nice, Katie. Katie, bring me a vase. No. No. I'll get it. I'll get it. John, give Katie your coat. No. Give me your coat. I'll take your coat. Wait a minute. You don't have a coat. Give me the flowers. Thank you. Thank you for the flowers."

"Mommy, you're talking all funny."

"Am I? I guess I am."

"Katie, did I introduce you? This is John."

"Hi, Katie."

"Oh god, I'm making a fool out of myself."

"No, you're not. No. You never would do that. No. Please. No. I'm so very glad to see you, Emmy."

"I'm so very glad to see you, John."

"Mommy, who is he?"

"He's your daddy, Katie. He's your daddy."

Chapter 5

"Dennis Moore. Dennis Moore. I bet they call you Dinty Moore."

"No, sir, they do not."

"They do not. All right, Officer Moore it is," said Billy Reagan. Moore was still standing at semi-attention, and Reagan had not given him permission to sit.

"But I will tell you something. A story. Officer Moore. A story I have not thought of for many years. But seeing you makes me think of it. And I will inflict it on you.

"Years ago, when I was a lad, my parents took me to California. By train. Three days. My first trip ever further from Boston than Revere Park. To see my mother's little brother, the big success in the family, William Timothy McDiver, the screenwriter. I was named for him, of course.

"Hollywood. A studio. Western town. The Western streets. The saloon where they shot *High Noon*. The greatest thrill of my young life. Then Billy McDiver, the big screenwriter, takes us to the studio commissary for lunch. In walks the most handsome man I have ever seen or ever will see: Tyrone Power. Far more handsome in person than in the movies. Dazzling smile. Pitch-black hair. Bright blue eyes. Ruddy complexion. Shoulders as wide as the Charles River.

"He comes over to our table, obviously a setup by Uncle Billy, and says to me, 'So is this your namesake? It's Billy, is it?' That's all. That's all he says. That was enough. I'll never forget it. And to this day, I have never seen a man reminded me of Tyrone Power until this very moment. You remind me of him, Officer Moore. County Tyrone?"

"County Mayo."

"Well, whatever. Now, I'm looking at this promotion list, Officer Moore, and I'm looking at this grievance that you, as the president of the Sanasauk Police Department Police Federation, have filed, and it is to the effect that I have been remiss in not acting favorably upon these recommendations for transfers and promotions, the officers on the lists having completed all the necessary paperwork, passed the exams, passed the orals, etc., etc. Is that the gist of it?"

"Sir?"

"I mean, the grievance, as I understand it, is that I should promote these donkeys because they have been handpicked by the Fed as their reward for pounding in lawn signs and ringing doorbells for the Fed's candidates for the city council?"

"Sir, that's an insult."

"Good, I'm glad you took it as such. It was meant to be. No, I will not promote them. But then again, I will not take disciplinary action against them either. There are no slots open for sergeant nor for lieutenant. We currently have a ratio of four to one in sergeants to patrol personnel. We currently have a ratio of seven to one lieutenants to patrol personnel. That is far too many chiefs for the number of Indians. You're not of the Native American persuasion, are you, Officer Moore? I haven't offended you, have I?"

"No, sir."

"Good. These ethnic references. I make far too many of them. Get me in trouble someday. County Mayo, it is, right?"

"Yessir."

"Now, if I have not made myself clear, here it is: until the ratio of sergeants to patrol people is at least ten to one and until the ratio of lieutenants to patrol personnel is at least eighteen to one, Einstein himself, even if he was Aloyisios O'Einstein, could not snag a promotion in the Sanasauk Police Department. Got that? Deaths. Disabilities. Retirements. That's the ticket to promotion. We wait on the will of the Almighty. Got that?"

"Exceptional circumstances excepted, sir?"

"Of course. Heroic rescue. Daring arrest. Etc. Etc. Officer Eddie White who couldn't pass fifth grade arithmetic is now Sergeant

Edward White thanks to a couple of well-placed rounds. All right, you handsome, silver-tongued Irish devil, you've already chipped away at my iron resolve. Now get the fuck out of here before I give away the store."

"Yessir."

Moore left.

Reagan pushed a button under his desk, and Celeste came into his office.

"How was that?"

"Fine, sir."

"I mean except for the cursing. I know I do too much of that too, but we have to use the language the men understand. It's like a dialect, Celeste."

"Yes, sir."

"Well, you don't seem too happy about it."

"No, sir. I thought it went fine. You made your point. You made it very forcefully."

"Good. Do you remember, Celeste, when the Democratic candidate for president of the United States was Michael Dukakis?"

"Yes, sir."

"Do you know why he lost that election?"

"No, sir."

"It was when the Massachusetts Police Officers Association rejected Dukakis, their own governor—over my objections, of course—and endorsed George Herbert Walker Bush.

"That did it for Dukakis. That and the Willie Horton ad. Law and order. But Mr. Clinton understood that the voters and the police have different priorities. What voters care about is getting the scum off the streets. What cops care about is wages and working conditions. Cops know crime is here to stay, and they can't do a hell of a lot about it. That's the job. The crime rate is determined by economic conditions and race relations. What do cops really worry about? How the hell am I going to make my alimony payments and handle the mortgage and the orthodontist? Cops are working stiffs, not ideologues.

"Our esteemed president understood this, and the first thing he did when he was campaigning was to go to the Massachusetts Police Officers Association. He didn't promise to lock down all the Willie Hortons for life. He talked bread and butter. A man or woman risking their lives on the street should get a paycheck that faintly resembles what the entry-level help was getting down the street at the State Street Bank. Bingo. Endorsement. And with the cops for him, the voters figured, 'Well, he may be a Democrat, but at least he's not another wuss like Dukakis.'"

"Yes, sir."

"Politics. It's part of the job, Celeste. The Fed has started getting tough on these promotions and transfers. New era. The old dogs who got off on whumping their customers with nightsticks—I prefer not to call them Billy clubs for obvious reasons—are about gone. But budgets are not gone. We still have to watch the pennies. Go slow. Give 'em a wee something, but not too much."

"Yes, sir. What did we give them?"

"Ah, now I remember why I buzzed you. Celeste, reach out for Sergeant John Steinmetz. Let's give him a day or two to puzzle it out with his rabbi, Dinty Moore, and make it Friday afternoon before we reel him in."

Steinmetz showed up at the scheduled time, dress uniform freshly pressed. The waiting room had been stripped of any magazines or newspapers. Steinmetz spent half an hour staring at the wall before he was called in.

"Sergeant, you may be seated."

"Thank you, sir."

"In reviewing your file and in response to the eloquent plea by the president of the Sanasauk Police Federation, I am granting the request for transfer to plainclothes."

"Thank you, sir."

"You'll report to Captain Bremer in Quality of Life Offenses Monday at 1600."

"What!"

"Pardon me?"

"Vice! I requested a transfer to Burglary. I'd sooner the Bow and Arrows."

"Sergeant. You are being granted a transfer from uniform to plainclothes, a clear-cut advancement in your career. And your reference to the unarmed unit is improper."

"The unarmed unit is for drunks who can't be trusted to carry a piece."

"As I recall, you had a similar problem. A DUI, wasn't it?"

"Sir, respectfully, that was over seven years ago. I wasn't even on the job."

"Normally, that would be enough to bar you from the force."

"Sir, that was expunged on condition I take treatment."

"Ah, yes, the twelve steps and come to Jesus. Well, lucky you. Times have changed. You never would have made it today. MADD trumps AA."

"Sir, respectfully, Vice is not the place for me."

"Why? It says here you have recently gotten married, you have a new family, a lovely wife and daughter, you ought to be able to keep your hands off the freebies.

"In two years, I'll take you out, send you to school, put you in Burglary, you'll get your promotion to lieutenant, and you'll be set. That's not too arduous a path for a bright, ambitious young man."

"I don't really care to spend two years on the Crack Squad charming street hos and staking out the men's john at Moonshine."

"That isn't your decision, Sergeant."

"Why don't you turn off the bubble machine?"

"The bubble machine?"

"The intercom."

"Are you suggesting that our conversation is being recorded?"

"Sir, that thing has been around since Lyndon Johnson installed his. We're cops. Every cop in the department knows about it."

"Sergeant Steinmetz, you're being insubordinate."

"Have it your way. Okay. Let's rock and roll. Couple of months ago, the Fed sends me to the national convention in Washington. I did the el cheapo and had them bunk me with a couple of other el cheapos. One's from Boston. One's from New Haven. You know how

37

cops talk. Seems they have an idea about why you were promoting Harold J. Fishman, and then when he gets bounced and goes back, you come out—"

"Shut up."

Reagan pushed the buzzer under his desk, and Celeste came in.

"Celeste, it's Friday afternoon and far too lovely a day to wring the last hour of toil from you. The taxpayers will forgive me. I suggest you take the rest of the day off."

"I'm out of here."

"That you are. That you are…All right, son, let's hear the rest of it."

"Seems Mrs. Reagan had more on her mind going to New Haven than visiting her little brother. You wanted Fishman out of there, and when he gets chopped and comes back, you decided that if he wasn't going to put any serious miles between you, then you had to be the one to get out of there."

"Totally false. Vicious. Malicious gossip."

"Right."

"You have discussed this with Dinty Moore, I assume?"

"I have discussed this with no one."

"I have reviewed your record quite thoroughly, Sergeant Steinmetz, and I find a great deal that is worthy of further consideration. Here we have the report on the attempted arrest of the two suspects in Officer Hope's murder. An exceptional case. And in exceptional cases, exceptions may be made.

"I will grant your transfer to Burglary. As a penance for your insubordination, you will serve six months in what you call Vice. You will then attend the Southern Police Academy, take the full burglary pull, investigatory techniques, interrogation techniques, advanced criminal law, etc., etc. You'll retake the lute orals, pass, and be in Burglary in nine months."

"I already passed the orals. By now, I should be a lieutenant."

"Lieutenant. From locum tenens. Do you ever read Keegan, Sergeant? *The Mask of Command*? No? In further reviewing the files, I note that the path of the bullets that entered the bodies of the Hope killing suspects suggest that the poor fuckers were on their knees saying their prayers and filling their pants when they were shot."

"I'll take the six in Vice, but I want the promotion now. It won't hurt you any to give Dinty Moore at least one of his promotions."

"I also note that the ballistics report indicates that the rounds recovered from the bodies were fired by Officer White. You didn't fire. Why not?"

"It was all over by the time we got there."

"Perhaps. That leaves unanswered the question of your marksmanship. You'll go to the range, say, next week. If you requalify, I will certify your promotion."

"Thank you, sir."

"You'll like Burglary. It's one of our higher callings. Do you know the difference between an amateur and a professional?"

"No, sir."

"Look at the dresser drawers. If just the bottom drawer is pulled out, it's an amateur. The amateurs start at the top and work their way down, so they have to close every drawer to get at the next one. Takes time. The pros work from the bottom to the top because they never have to close a drawer."

"Yes, sir."

"Know where you can be sure you'll never be burglarized?"

"No, sir."

"When you live next door to a professional. They never foul their own nests, though, of course, they have been known to shit in other people's. Right in the middle of bed in the master bedroom. Another professional calling card."

"Yes, sir."

"Dismissed."

Steinmetz left.

Reagan made a phone call.

Chapter 6

Four years later

"If you were to commit murder, Inspector Donovan, what method would you use?"

"Depends, Chief. If it were a random deal, you know, just for the thrill of it, I'd probably do it like the Hillside Stranglers. Just pick up a ho, do her with a piece of rope from the Wal-Mart, and toss her in the bushes."

"But what if it were someone we could connect you with?"

"Well, then it gets a bit more complicated. What do you suggest?"

"What I'm suggesting is that Zeno Malkin may have had some assistance in taking the high dive. Very, very hard to prove a fall. Forensics of no help. Body's a total mess. Smart lawyer can explain away every tiny scratch."

"Chief, why are we having this conversation? I can handle this, believe me. That's why you put me head of Homicide."

Reagan ignored the question.

"We had a case once in Boston. Even more high profile than this one. Of national interest. Before your time, so you wouldn't remember. Joshua Stern. Big, big businessman. President of the world's biggest fruit company. They owned the plantations. They owned the ships. They owned the port facilities. There had been investigations. He had been bribing all these tinhorn Central American politicians, of course. Nothing new in that. But he'd been cooking his books too. One fine day, he's up in his lofty perch atop the corporate headquarters, beautiful view of Boston harbor, where all his pineapples and bananas come in, and he decides to take the leap. Well, he can't get the damn window open, because of course the windows in these new office towers don't open. They're sealed into their frames. He bangs away at it with an ashtray. No go. Finally, he fills up his briefcase with stuff, ashtrays, awards, paperweights, a coconut he keeps on his desk, knocks out a hole, and walks out the window, still holding the briefcase.

"I understand when they found Zeno, what he was holding onto was his Johnson."

"Our shrink consultant tells me that's not unusual in these cases, something about 'It's the only thing they've got left to hang onto.'"

"He landed on his back."

"Not all that unusual either. Some of them would rather take that last look at the sky than at the sidewalk coming at them."

"Eight at night?"

"Still some light. Sunset at eight twenty-one."

"No note?"

"No note."

"Office staff all gone, I presume."

"Yeah, door to the office locked."

"Could he have opened it to let someone in, and then the someone does him, leaves and locks it behind them?"

"Not unless they had a key, Chief. Dead-bolt lock. You need a key to lock it from the outside. We had to get the super to let us in."

"So no burglar trying unlocked doors. No break-in. If someone did him, they had to have had a key. Locked it on the way out thinking to make it look more like a suicide. Did Zeno's key turn up?"

"Yeah. He had it on him."

"How did he break the window?"

"Pushed his desk up close to the window, sat on the ledge with his back on the glass, pushed on the desk really hard, the frame gave, and out he went."

"Ejaculate?"

"Yeah, there was still a little bit on the tip."

"Where did the rest of it go?"

"Didn't find any."

"Maybe it wound up in someone's mouth. Did him while he was leaning against the window and then threw him against it, and he's airborne with his pecker flapping in the wind."

"Forensics says it's not unusual for ejaculate to be present."

"Do you like anybody?"

"Zeno had a couple thousand nonfriends. He made a few more with his latest scam. There's this penny gold stock, Brazama Gold. Name comes from Brazil and Amazon. Zeno goes to the offices, a walk-up over a drugstore. There's a couple of guys sitting around playing gin and waiting for the mail to come in so they can charge the brokers a $5 transfer fee for every ownership change on the stock. Zeno plops a bag on the desk. There's $50,000 cash in it and a clear sealed plastic tube about six inches around and a foot long filled with mud and water."

"A core sample."

"Right. Zeno holds it up to the light. There's little flecks of gold in it. He says, 'A geologist friend of mine says he got this from your claim on the Amazon. If we can get a dredge upriver, the claim is worth gazillions. I'll give you $50,000 for an option to buy two million shares of the stock at a dollar a share.'

"The stock's selling a little higher than usual at the time, about twenty-five cents a share, and here this guy is offering to pay fifty large cash for the right to buy it at a buck. Must be something there. So they go for it. Send out a letter to their shareholders, explain the deal, with a picture of the dredge, looks like a giant cockroach with these cranes sprouting out of it in all directions."

"The stock goes up."

"The stock goes up. Twenty-five cents. Fifty cents. Seventy-five cents. Zeno sends the Brazama boys the progress reports. They send out more letters to their shareholders. The barge is heading out of Miami down the coast. The barge has entered the mouth of the Amazon. The barge is heading up the tributary chopping its way to the claim. The stock gets to ninety cents. Bam, it turns around and goes down. Bam. Bam. Bam. We're back where we started. The Brazama boys call Zeno. What happened? 'Well,' says Zeno, 'we tried to get the barge upriver, got all tangled up in the weeds, couldn't make it. Sorry. So I guess we won't be exercising our option. But you got fifty grand for your trouble."

"What's the hustle?"

"Zeno and a favored few buy the stock at up to twenty-five cents a share, just tons and tons of it. Makes his deal with the Brazama boys. Sells it on the way up at seventy-five cents for a three-bagger, and probably shorts it on the way down. The barge? Some old rust bucket they sent down there so nobody could say they didn't try. All perfectly legal unless you can prove fraud, that Zeno never *intended* to dredge out the claim. The fifty grand for the option was just an expense, like the cost of the nuggets when you're salting a mine. They probably cleared upwards of a million and left two three hundred people holding the bag. Last I heard the stock was down to a nickel, and the Brazilian government was expropriating the claim for non-payment of taxes. The Brazama boys were telling their stockholders to write their congressman."

"Old joke: What's a gold mine? A hole in the ground with a liar on top."

"We got a shareholders list from the Brazama boys. There are about fifty locals in it. Four or five big losers of about thirty grand each."

"Stockholders don't kill, they sue. Any other ideas?"

"The usual, wife, girlfriends, jealous boyfriends. I don't like the ladies because I don't see them tossing around desks and a hundred-eighty-pound tub of guts."

"Agreed, Inspector. Okay, it's a guy with a key. Why would the key guy show at seven or eight after everyone has left? Zeno doesn't strike me as a workaholic. It's someone Zeno didn't want anyone else to see. Anyone sign in downstairs with security?"

"Nope."

"How did he get past them?"

"Oh, lots of ways. This isn't exactly the boom-boom room at missile launch headquarters. Could have waited outside until the guy at the desk went for a pee. Could have slipped into the garage behind a car then climbed the stairs. Could have been sitting in the can. Could have gotten a pass card from Zeno to park in the garage."

"No. He wouldn't have used a pass card. The car would stand out. Just about everyone else has gone home. But check with security just to be sure. Was Zeno gay?"

"Not that we're aware of. But some of these guys are plenty good at keeping it quiet."

"Do me this. Try the gay angle. Anyone he may have known who was gay—and had a motive."

"If they knew Zeno, they had a motive."

Two months later, Inspector Donovan called Reagan.

"I got something on the Malkin space walk. Want to do this on the phone?"

"Hell, no. This is the House of Whispers. Come on in."

He was sitting across from Reagan within the hour.

"Okay, Chief, we run all the names on the Malkin list through the computer, see if any of them have a record. Nothing but traffic stuff. Then, based on our conversation a couple of months ago, Detectives Hanlon and Willie Jefferson on my squad get copied on all sodomy reports. Any name appears on one of those gets cross-checked against any name we got on the Malkin lists. Last week, one Franklin D. Simms is arrested while playing the skin flute in one of the stalls at Moonshine. Name of Franklin D. Simms appears in the acknowledgments of *Malkin the Falcon*. This a long list of close personal friends of the author who inspired him to undertake his literary efforts, including the pope, the secretary general of the United Nations, Joe DiMaggio, Larry King, etc., etc. Anyway, the name Franklin D. Sims sticks out a bit in that company, so we do some checking.

"One, Simms didn't have a key, not that we know about, based on the records Zeno's secretary kept. But that doesn't mean Zeno may not have given him one and not wanted anyone to be aware of it. Two, even if Zeno did give him a key, guys doing it to guys in private isn't a crime, it's a lifestyle. And Simms may have had a legitimate business reason for having a private meeting with Zeno. We think he may have been the guy who ghosted most of Zeno's stuff, and Zeno liked to keep that very quiet. Zeno wanted the world to think he actually wrote it, though I doubt if he could have written *My Summer Vacation* by himself."

"What makes you think he was Zeno's ghost?"

"What we have here is a high school English teacher with a net worth of over six hundred thousand bucks with a connection of some sort to one of our nation's best-selling authors."

"I take it you fished those financial statements out of Franklin's trash can since no bank or stock broker would give them to you without a court order."

"Yeah, well, let's just say in this business, you have to have friends in high places. If this goes any further, I'll cover our asses with a court order."

"No. You'll cover your ass. My ass is covering this chair, and that's where it stays."

"Yeah, okay, Chief. Anyway, that's about where we're at."

"I take it you haven't talked to Simms yet."

"I got the feeling from the last time you wanted some input first."

"Okay, Inspector, before we get all excited, let's review what we got. The double connection, if it exists, writer of words and giver of head, is both good news and bad news. The ghost thing gives him a reason to be there after hours, do his business and leave. If he was the ghost. The gay thing may also be the reason he was there on the sly, did his business, and went on his way. But we don't know if Zeno was gay. And neither one is a motive to commit murder, just a reason to meet after hours. And we don't know that he was there.

"The money is also a good thing and a bad thing. It strengthens the ghost possibility but weakens the motive. He's got six hundred thousand bucks. If he didn't inherit it, maybe he got it from Zeno. Why kill the goose that lays the golden eggs?

"So, Homicide Inspector Donovan, we have no motive, we're a little weak on opportunity, since we lack the key and anything but a hunch to put Franklin at the scene.

"That leaves the means. We think it's possible Zeno got thrown through a window. A sealed window. But maybe even the dumbass freak governor they've got in Minnesota couldn't throw someone through that window. What have you got on that?"

"We're not in bad shape there. Building put up on spec during the nineties construction boom. Seals are bad. Every time there's a breeze, one of the windows blows out and falls on a pedestrian. Besides, a little more on our friend Franklin. He's not just an English teacher. He's the wrestling coach. Fitness freak. Got to stay buffed if you want to make new friends in his crowd. He could handle Zeno easy."

"I'm beginning to like Franklin. How many people had keys?"

"You mean that we're sure of? The secretary's list shows five names. We've checked them all out. Nothing there."

"If Simms had a key, do you think he was smart enough to get rid of it?"

"Who knows? What if I send a couple of guys over to see him on the sodomy thing? One guy keeps him busy while the other guy pokes around."

"No. If Simms has still got it, I don't want to do anything to spook him. No cop is going to show face until we know if he's got it."

"Okay, what if we send a nice little coppette over, all dressed up in a Community Protection Corps outfit. She's in the neighborhood because there's been a rash of burglaries in the area, has he got one of those new burglarproof double-tooth lock and key sets? Lemme see your key, I'll show you how easy it is to pick the regular lock. Checks out the key chain."

"No. What if it's stashed and not on the key chain? I don't want to breathe the word *key* around this guy until we know if he's got it. And I want to take care of the sodomy charge before the school finds out about it. I don't want him leaving town or hanging himself from the shower rod just yet. So go to the city attorney, get him to prepare some kind of bullshit letter, 'No charge will be pursued at this time pending further investigation. You will be notified if there's any change,' blah, blah. That way, we can always reactivate it if we need it."

"What if we toss the place, Chief? We'll do it real messy. Maybe we find something. Even if we don't, we see if he reports it. If he's too scared to call us, that tells me he doesn't want anything to do with us."

"No. It doesn't tell us if he's got the key if he's carrying it around with him, and even if we do find it, we can't take it, and he may spook and throw it away."

"Okay, Chief, I got a way to do this, check out the key chain without Simms knowing about it. Let's call it plan A. If Plan A doesn't produce, then we go to plan B, toss the place very professionally, he'll never know it, and if we find it, we get the court order."

"You need probable cause for a court order."

"Old Rumsy doesn't set the bar too high, ever since we opened the wrong door at Lady Lil's."

"Okay, I approve Plan B. Care to tell me who you're going to use to toss the place?"

"Steinmetz. Lute. Very smooth operator. Simms will never know he was there."

"I've heard of him. Care to tell me about Plan A?"

"Chief, I understand the drill: Simms is not to know we're on his case. I don't think you want to know the rest."

"I think what you think. Have a nice day."

"You have a nice day too, Chief."

CHAPTER 7

Franklin Simms was too upset to notice that his car was being followed. The windshield of his green Mazda had been smashed by a crowbar, leaving a massive, nearly opaque blot of splintered glass directly atop the driver's sightline and spreading out in a spiderweb of fractures and cracks. Simms crept along the side streets, cursing the vandals who had done it and caused him to miss his first class.

He pulled into Premier Auto Glass Repair, called his insurance company, made arrangements to pick up the car after work, handed his keys to the attendant at the service desk, and headed for the bus stop.

A half an hour after Simms had caught his bus, a brown Chrysler with a similarly bashed-in windshield pulled into the same repair shop and, minus the call to the insurance company, made arrangements for a replacement. An hour after that, two plainclothes policemen arrived. After they identified themselves to the attendant as Detectives Hanlon and Jefferson, Detective Jefferson announced the purpose of their visit.

"We got an anonymous tip about an hour ago, said you guys might be servicing stolen cars here. We gotta check out licenses, registrations, every car in the shop," said Detective Willie Jefferson, consulting a clipboard that had a Stolen Vehicle flyer on top with a description of the Chrysler on it.

"Hey, Detective Jefferson, isn't that the brown Chrysler on our list?" said Hanlon.

"I believe it sure is, Detective Hanlon. Will you please check it out for me. Pardon me, mister…mister? I didn't catch the name?"

"Dan. Just call me Dan."

"Sewed right on your shirt, isn't it? Some detective I am. Well, thank you Jesus for affirmative action. No objections to our looking around, I trust?"

"Oh, no, sir, that fellow that brought that in about an hour ago, I never seen him before. He just walked off, heading east. Said he'd be back around closing time."

"Closing time. Well, you'll never see him again, Dan. He'll drive by later on with one of his buddies, kind of scope out the place…Say, Detective Hanlon, when you're through with that Chrysler, check out that green Mazda they've got in that work station over there, will you? I think that's one of them too…Well, as I was saying, Dan, he'll drive by here with an accomplice a little before closing, make sure there's nothing funny going on, and then if the coast is clear, they'll bop in and say, Dan, was the guy about five foot ten, Caucasian guy, about one hundred seventy pounds, about thirty, dark hair, brown eyes? He was, huh? I thought so. That's our guy. That's the guy we're looking for, Dan…Pardon me. Anything, Detective Hanlon?"

"Nah, clean as a whistle. Nothing. Key chain. Glove compartment. Under the seat. Under the dash. Nothing."

"In other words, the car is not on our list?"

"Nope. Not on our list."

"Well, my mistake. I don't see anything else here that might be on our list except that brown Chrysler… Ah, here's the police tow now…Good thing we got here right away, Dan. If you'd started working on it, you might never gotten paid."

"Who gave you the tip?"

"Sounded like an angry girlfriend to me. These guys treat their women like shit, Dan."

"But what happens when the guy shows up?"

"Dan, he ain't never showing up. You have seen the last of that scumbag. When he drives by with his accomplice and sees the car isn't here, he'll just keep on going. But you're worried about anything, or if he does show, just try and stall him and give me a call. Here's my card."

"Detective Jefferson. It says Homicide."

"That's my old card. That's okay. I can still be reached at the same number. Say, Dan, I wouldn't mention our little visit to any of your other customers. Might make them nervous, not want to do business here. Well, adios, Dan...Hey, tow guy. Impound lot, right?"

The police tow returned the stolen car to the impound lot from where it had been signed out that morning. Jefferson and Hanlon caught up with the driver of the Chrysler at a Hardees about a ten-minute walk from Premier Auto Glass.

"It looks like it's your turn, Steinmetz," said Hanlon. "He didn't have it on his key chain, and it wasn't in the car."

Steinmetz grunted and finished his coffee.

"How about a lift? Drop me off about a block or two from Simms's place, say, Eighteenth and Buchanan?" said Steinmetz.

"Want us to wait for you outside in case he shows up?"

"Nah, he's teaching school. No problemo. Piece of cake."

"Ready?"

"Always."

Simms lived in an inner-city development of twenty row houses which originally had been nineteenth railroad workers' cottages and had been gentrified in the 1980s. Each was free-standing, separated from its neighbors by a discreet distance, though there were no fences between them. There were ten on one side of what once had been a street and ten on the other side. The street had been filled in, and the cottages now faced each other across what was now a grassy mall with a gently winding sidewalk and few benches. The garages were separate and behind the houses. Most of the cottages, including Simms's, were A-frames, with lofts for bedrooms, and a main floor atrium in which living, dining, and kitchen areas flowed into each other, loosely separated by half walls.

Simms had lined one wall of his living area with bookshelves, which reached up to the loft. A library ladder on rollers leaned against the shelves, the only way the higher shelves were accessible. There were at least a thousand books.

Steinmetz entered by picking the back door lock. He groaned when he saw the bookshelves.

He needn't have. Simms had hidden the key in the standard place for hiding keys: taped under a dresser drawer. Steinmetz checked the pattern against his copy to make sure it was the same and left Simms's key where he had found it, undisturbed.

He scanned the library. There didn't appear to be any gay material, though he only checked under a dozen or so dust jackets. The only books of interest were signed copies of Zeno's books, with inscriptions thanking Franklin for his "wise counsel and inspiration," his "friendship and loyal support," but no direct reference to his having actually written them.

From the absence of any gay-oriented materials, Steinmetz gathered that Simms probably had students visit from time to time and wanted nothing openly visible on the premises that could compromise him at the school. There was a PC in a hutch against the wall that abutted the library shelves. Steinmetz booted it up, waited for the prompt to ask for the password, felt under the slide-out board that held the keyboard, and found a Post-It note with Simms's password and PIN. Steinmetz logged onto Simms's word processing program and scanned the entries. He found manuscript versions of Zeno's books, with lengthy addendums and revisions, and additions and subtractions and memos to Zeno, some benign, some relatively heated as Simms argued for or against this or that editorial incursion by Zeno. He checked the email and some of the more popular gay sites, but there was nothing.

A professional burglar never takes more than seven minutes max. Steinmetz had taken forty. He logged off and got out.

*****

"Congratulations," said Reagan to Donovan.

"Yeah, thanks," said Donovan.

"Okay, let's bring Simms in on Saturday. Wait until he drives into the parking lot to do his grocery shopping, so no Fudgicles melting in the back seat. Tell him the city attorney wants us to clear up this Moonshine thing. Real low-key. One person, not the SWAT team. Make it Jefferson, driving his private vehicle, not a battle wagon. If

Simms gets nasty, have Jefferson tell him we're being nice so we don't embarrass him. We can always wait until Monday and arrest him at school in front of his whole class. He'll go. Have Jefferson tell him to follow him down here in his own car. Let Simms think it's just a bullshit thing and he's still in control, and he'll be back snafing down those Fudgicles in a few minutes.

"While this is going on, paste Rumsy's order on Simms's front door, go in messy, bring back the key, and make sure there's some other stuff, anything else that looks interesting. Now let me see that order."

Donovan handed him the draft of the search warrant.

"Good. Nice and vague. No mention of the key. Put a dummy key there after you take Simms's. If we got to release him, I don't want him to know we've got it until we decide to tell him.

"Now, here's the program: Jefferson reels him in. Jefferson does the interrogation. Alone. They'll be in the Romper Room. We'll watch. We got means, we got opportunity, we got motive, kind of, some gay thing, or money thing probably. Let's see what he can pry loose. What we no got is proof. No proof whatsoever. No DNA. No fibers. No weapon. No nothing. So if this is going to go down, Jefferson has got to find a way to make Simms give it up. Now go do it."

By the time Jefferson and Simms got settled into the interrogation room, Simms was a total, nearly incoherent mess.

"I am not gay. I am not gay. This was not me. I do not do these things. I have never done this kind of thing."

"Mr. Simms, Mr. Simms, sir. Sir. Please. Listen to me. Now listen to me. Listen to me carefully. I'm sure we can clear this up. No one wants to hurt you, Mr. Simms."

"My father would kill me. He would kill me. My mother. Thank god she's dead. I am sitting thanking God my mother is dead. I wish I was dead."

"Mr. Sims, please. No one wants you dead. No one wants to hurt you. Mr. Simms, your father, your father is not going to hurt you. We're not going to let your father hurt you, Mr. Simms."

"I thought this was all over. I got this letter from the city attorney. He said they weren't prosecuting. They said they made a mistake. It was all over. If there was any change, they'd let me know."

"Mr. Simms, I have a copy of the letter. Here's a copy of the letter. It says, 'There will be no charges filed at this time pending further investigation.' Pending further investigation, Mr. Simms. That's this. That's what we're doing now. I'm getting your version. I want to know your side of the story, Mr. Simms. Tell me. What happened, Mr. Simms?"

"That fucker turned me out. I have never, never ever had a homosexual experience. There were times I could have. I was at summer camp once. I was only nine or ten, and this counselor tried something. Well, he didn't try it. He just talked about it, and I said, 'If anyone here ever tried that on me, I'd go right to the camp director.' Boy, that was that. He was the photography guy. We were in the darkroom when he started in on that. Boy, did the lights ever go on in a hurry."

"Who turned you out?"

"No one."

"You said 'that fucker turned me out.'"

"I don't know. I don't know what I'm saying. This is all horrible. I've never been in a police station in my life. I want to go home."

"Of course, of course. Let's just clear this up first. You don't want this hanging over your head the rest of your life. I need to know what happened so we can clear this up. Tell me what happened."

"Nothing happened. I never did anything."

"Mr. Simms, Mr. Simms, I'm a reasonable man. I have a sympathetic view of the human condition. People in my job see horrible things, terrible things. This is not a horrible, terrible thing. This is a human thing. These things happen. Things like this can happen to anyone. We have too much to drink. Our defenses are down. We meet someone who's attractive. We want to please them. The next thing you know, whammo, we're being used. It can happen. Now tell me. What happened here?"

"I was used. I was used by a horrible, horrible man. Not just sex. He used me in even worse ways. He took away my identity. He took away my being. He took everything away and twisted and changed it and made it into his own and threw me away. It wasn't sex. It wasn't about sex. I'm not gay. I don't want anyone ever to say that I'm a homosexual. I'm not. I can get all kinds of women to say I'm not. Lots of women. I've had hundreds of women."

"Well, let's drop this gay thing for now. Do you want to do that? Talk about something else?"

"Yes."

"Maybe you can help us with another matter. If you can help us there, maybe we can help you. Do you want to try and help us so we can help you, Mr. Simms? Would you like that?"

"Yes."

"You know, you are obviously a very intelligent, very talented person. You are a teacher. I've always admired teachers very much. I would not be here today if my high school English teacher had not taken an interest in me, encouraged me to make something of myself, helped get me financial aid so I could go to SU. I was the first person in my family ever to go to college. My mom, well, it was the proudest day of her life, day I got that diploma. If it hadn't been for my teacher, name of Mr. Hamid Rashid Mohammed, you find me dealing crack on some street corner in South Sanasauk or dead or in prison. So I have great admiration for what you have accomplished. And then I read these motivational books, keep me sharp and keep the juices flowing, it's not so easy doing what I do either, and I see your name on those too…"

Jefferson reached into his briefcase and pulled out a copy of *Malkin the Falcon* and pushed it across the table. Simms stared at it as if it carried the plague. "Acknowledgments. Many people have helped in the preparation of this work. Without their counsel, their wisdom, their friendship and support, the book you are about to read would not have been possible. And there it is, your name, Franklin Simms, right between Mohammed Ali and Henry Kissinger.' You must have made an enormous contribution to—"

"That rotten, lying cocksucker took everything and twisted it, twisted it, changed it, pissed on it, shit on it. He was not permitted, not allowed to change my copy, not change a comma, without asking me first. The only reason he finally put my name in one of those goddamn books was because I raised such a stink about it he finally had to give me some credit or I would have had a press conference and blown his phony ass right out of the water."

"He changed your copy?"

"Yes. He changed it. He had no right to change it."

"Is that why you—"

"Oh, let's get this fucking thing over with. Yes. That's why."

"Mr. Simms, I am placing you under arrest for the murder of Zeno Malkin. I have to inform you that…"

Watching through the one-way glass with two other cops, Reagan wore a thin smile. He shook his head in wonderment.

"Jesus. Twenty-five years on the job and it's still a mystery, some of them, you got them dead to rights, fingerprints, DNA, the whole megillah, and they still find a way to run through the tiniest opening, give you the finger and they're off to the golf course the rest of their lives.

"This one, you bust your ass for three months laying the groundwork, setting it up, sweating the holes in your story, and none of it matters. He would have popped if we'd brought him in the day we heard his name. And we got the motive wrong. A bad edit. Well, they say 'The editor is to the author as the knife is to the throat.' I guess Simms believed it. Doesn't really change anything though, does it, lad?"

"No, sir, but I don't think that's why he did it, sir," said Steinmetz, not knowing what he was doing there with the chief and a captain. "I think he killed Zeno for turning him out. Zeno made him see himself in a way he didn't want to."

Reagan ignored the comment and turned to the other officer.

"So, Captain Jefferson, did you fail to attend your son's graduation?"

"He didn't say I *didn't* attend, Chief. He just said his mother was there. Lots of white folks don't think we have fathers. Willie didn't want to distract the perp at the moment of truth. I did attend, and his English teacher's name was Mildred Thatcher, not Hamid whatever."

"A gifted storyteller, our William," said Reagan, turning back to Steinmetz. "Well, lad, what did you think of our man Detective Jefferson? Want to try your hand at homicide?"

"No, sir," said Steinmetz. "Too much bullshit for me. I want to go back to the street."

*****

The backup parked in the alley beside the first squad car, and two men got out. One went over to the body in the snowbank. The other went over to the man with the shotgun.

"What happened, Eddie?" said Steinmetz.

"Driving through the alley, heard the screaming, pulled in. Called for backup. Stepped out. He must've heard me, gone out on the back porch. I see kind of a glint. I think maybe's there's something in his hand.

"Porch light on or off?"

"Off."

"You're absolutely sure?

"Yeah."

"Then what?"

"Duck back in the squad. Get the shotgun. Steady it behind the car door. I say, 'Police. Put down your gun.'"

"Ah yes, 'pulueese.' Oh well, who's to know. Yeah, then what?"

"I dunno."

"C'mon, Eddie, you know better than that? He had a piece, right? He fired at you, right?"

"Jesus, have you got one? I don't have anything. At least I took care of his hands."

"Eddie, guess what? I'm looking over there in the snowbank, and I think I see a piece. I think maybe he fired at you twice. Well?"

"Yeah, yeah, I suppose."

"No, Eddie, no supposing. You gotta be sure. Are you sure?"

"Yeah, I'm sure."

"Then you fired, right?"

"Right."

"Okay, I gotta call that prick Donovan in Homicide. She still upstairs?"

"I suppose so."

"Okay, now I'm going back to my squad for a second, call Donovan, then I'm going to check on that piece in the snowbank, then I gotta go upstairs, calm her down. Now, take the shotgun, put it on safe, lean it against my squad...Okay, give me your piece. Now, wait until I'm through calling Donovan, then go sit in my squad. In the back. Got it? It'll be okay, Eddie."

"Hey, John," said the other officer. "You'll never believe who this is?"

"Who?"

"It's Witherspoon."

CHAPTER 8

"Thank you for taking the time to see me, sir," said Reagan.

"Chief, in the history of New York City, do you know how many successful homicide prosecutions there have been of police officers on duty killing civilians?" said County Attorney Wilson Barlow.

"No, but I have a feeling you're going to tell me," said Reagan.

"Three. In over two hundred years. Three."

"This isn't New York City."

"No, it isn't. New York has 8,800 cops. We have 1,200."

"And this isn't a civilian. It's a cop killing another cop."

"Witherspoon was not a cop, Chief. He was an ex-cop, a psycho ex-cop stomping a hooker and waving around a handgun."

"And you're sure she'll testify that way? And the handgun?"

"Answer to question one: yes. We've interviewed her. Answer to question two: your ballistics boys are not finished yet, but I doubt if you can show it's a throwdown."

"Mr. Barlow, re Gloria Two Bears, the lady of the evening. She's got a rap sheet longer than a giant roll of Charmin Plus but nothing in the last year and a half. Eddie White spent four years on Vice. That's a long stretch on the pussy patrol unless you really like the action. Could Gloria and our putative defendant have an arrangement?"

"Sure, she could owe him a favor. Of course, but proving it is another matter."

"Do you really think Witherspoon was standing out on that porch in thirty-degree weather in his shorts carrying a handgun?"

"Chief, he's a certified psycho. Discharged three years ago for firing his gun in a public place. Apparently fun with guns is his MO."

"Certified psycho. Reminds me of a story. First time George Wallace runs for governor of Alabama, his opponent says Wallace is nuts. Turns out Wallace was a tail gunner during the war, got shaken up, spent a little time in the hospital, gets a ten percent disability for nervous disorder. Wallace loses the election. Next time Wallace runs, of course they're still saying he's nuts, so he gets up and waves around his medical discharge. 'I'm the only one in this election that's ninety percent sane, and I got a certificate to prove it.' This time he wins."

"What's the point, Chief?"

"The point is that Witherspoon's nuttiness is not a minus, it's a plus. I want to get back to you again when that ballistics report comes down."

Three weeks later, Reagan was in Barlow's office again.

"You've read it, I trust?" said Reagan.

"Yes."

"You agree that it's a throwdown."

"Yes."

"May I tell you what I think happened."

"Certainly, Chief. That's why you're here."

"Okay. It's a setup. White circles the block for a while. Gloria's door is ajar, so sound carries, but Witherspoon is too drunk to notice. She starts yelling and screaming and throwing stuff around before he can get off. That's the signal. White pulls up. Calls him out. Witherspoon hears his name, steps out on the porch. White blows him away. Calls the backup. They're on top of him before he has a chance to fire the throwaway, and now he's afraid they'll hear it if he fires. So he checks the cylinder, sees that its full, spent cartridges already in it, dumps all but two into his pocket, and throws it in a puddle. Then he buries Witherspoon's hands in that wet snow to gaff the powder burn test, and by that time, Steinmetz and Olson are there."

"Chief, this ain't TV. Even if it's a throwdown, that doesn't mean a jury is going to convict him of murder. Not a cop. I don't mean to raise unpleasantries here, but you know you are not the most popular guy in the world with the rank and file. Union busting is not a great way to foster labor relations in Sanasauk."

"Cops do not have the right to strike. You're the lawyer. You know that better than I do. I can understand the mayor may not want to get tough, but I don't have his situation. I don't have to run for election. And I'm not going to lay down just to keep this job."

"We're in a powder keg here."

"We're in a wages-and-working-conditions dispute, and we're in a murder investigation. In my opinion, and it's just an opinion, I think we got to deal with them as separate issues."

"What do you want here?"

"Murder one."

"I'm going to give it to you, and I don't have to tell you a cute story about what happens when you get what you want. God help you. I'll give the file to Emily Steinmetz."

"Wait. Let's not be too hasty here. Her ex is going to be a witness."

"So? Lots of exes wind up in court on opposite sides, Chief."

"Who said they're going to be on opposite sides?"

"You think he'll testify for us? For her?"

"I think he knows the whole story from day one. And I think it's tearing him apart."

*****

Reagan walked down the two flights of stairs from Barlow's office to his own and called Donovan.

"Okay, Ray, I sold your case to Barlow. It's your baby now," said Reagan.

"I need another favor, Chief," said Donovan.

"What?"

"I want a travel voucher. See Guiterrez. Mexico City."

"What do you think she's going to tell you?"

"The truth, I hope."

"Even if she does, you don't expect her to come back for the trial, do you?"

"No."

"Can you take a deposition down there?"

"Maybe, who knows, but it wouldn't be worth shit anyway, so why bother. I just want her to tell me what really happened."

"Worth a try. Who you sending?"

"Me."

"You don't really trust anyone, do you? An admirable trait in our profession."

"This is a cop thing, Chief, and you know it. Cop versus cop versus cop. And no, I don't really trust anyone. The first thing old Francis Bailey tells me when I come aboard this squad is, 'Remember, whenever anyone tells you anything, and that includes your brothers in blue, the number one question you got to ask yourself is, "Why is this sonofabitch lying to me."'"

"Have a nice trip, son."

Donovan had been somewhat surprised when Ramona Guiterrez agreed to meet with him. She had resigned from the force about a year after the cornfield shootings. Her husband, who had started his career as an assembly line worker at the VW plant, Sanasauk's largest employer, had worked his way up through the ranks to management and been transferred to an executive position with VW in Mexico City.

Ambitious and tireless, Manny Guiterrez had taken night courses in automotive engineering, economics, management, German, and modern European history at Sanasauk University for ten years while never missing a day of work. He always had wanted an overseas assignment, but he thought it would be Wolfsburg, not Latin America. As a third generation Chicano, Manny didn't speak any more Spanish than your average Sanasaukian Jew speaks Hebrew, but after two years of the Mexican executive lifestyle, he knew he would never want to leave.

Ramana was even more certain that they had landed in paradise. No more ugly uniforms, ugly people, eighty-mile-an-hour car chases, being called a *puta*, spat on, used in a hundred different horrible ways. Now her home was a villa, with servants and flowers and a swimming pool, not a cookie-cutter bungalow in a treeless suburb. She was a lady. Protected. Pampered. An object of respect. Almost veneration.

<<missing page 108>>

brimmed hat. She had put on about ten pounds, but ampleness was becoming to her. She was a strikingly handsome woman.

"Senora Guiterrez, I presume," said Donovan, smiling broadly.

"Captain Donovan."

"Ah, but it's Inspector now. Head of the whole schmear."

"Congratulations."

"Thanks. So who do I like in the feature race?"

"Our horse is Tarry This Night. The race is a mile and a sixteenth. She comes from off the pace, and it's a long way from the last turn to the finish, so she has a good shot."

"Long home stretch kills speed, is that the idea?"

"You've done this before."

"Born and raised in New Orleans. The Fair Grounds. Longest home stretch in America, 1,346 feet. Front runners die before your very eyes. You pick the Bible name for the horse?"

"Knows his horses. Knows his Bible. Yes. We bought her last spring at the Keeneland two-year-olds in training sale at Lexington. By Green Dancer out of a stakes placed Raise A Native mare."

"I don't know the Bible all that well, but I've always loved the book of Ruth. Not the first part so much, with the 'Wither thou goest,' but the last part with Boaz and Naomi, where the old man asks her to spend the night. 'Tarry this night.' Greatest seduction line of all time. Wish I'd had the chance to use it sometime."

"I heard."

"About the trial."

"Yeah."

"Are you going to tell me what happened that night?"

"No."

"There are some appropriate passages from the Bible I could quote here."

"Don't."

"You know, Senora Guiterrez, we are not Unitarians. There is a God. He makes judgments. Everything is not compassion and forgiveness. There is reckoning. There is a price for sin. All the flowers and perfume cannot blot out the stench. Prancing horses cannot hide it."

"Why don't you get the fuck out of here and go home."

"I'm not asking you to testify. I don't want you to testify. I don't want you come back with me. You wouldn't do it anyway, and I can't make you do it. Just tell me the truth."

"I can't."

"Why?"

"I just can't."

"Senora Guiterrez, I don't care about what you may have done back there. I can guess some parts of it. Would it be all right if you just let me talk a bit? You don't have to say anything, just nod."

Tears were streaming down her face.

"Why did I let you come here?"

"Because we believe in God, Ramona, and we know he waits and waits for us to do the right thing." She says nothing. Donovan began talking again.

"You and Samuel are a couple of blocks off the freeway. The dispatcher alerts all units in the area to join in the chase. Okay so far?"

She does not nod.

"Okay so far?"

She nods.

"You come in right behind White. Steinmetz is the caboose a ways back. When the truck spins out, you and White are practically on top of them. The two guys get out of the truck, start running. Sam and Eddie are chasing them. But Sam is a former high school athlete, a track star, and Eddie is a fat slob. Sam runs them down and holds them at gunpoint. About five seconds later, Eddie catches up. Am I doing all right?" She nods.

"Now you get there, and then Steinmetz. Then—"

"Steinmetz gets there before I do. I really don't see what happens next."

"What happens next is that Eddie smokes them. They're down on their fucking knees, two black guys shitting their pants, begging for their lives, another black guy, a cop, begging Eddie not to shoot, and Eddie says 'Fuck you' and gives them each a pop in the chest."

"I told you, I really didn't see it. I didn't get there until it was all over. Steinmetz was there. He saw what happened."

"All right, Senora Guiterrez, just tell me this. Tell me what Samuel did. Tell me what his reaction was to all this."

She started crying again, but this time, not quietly. Large, guttural sobs. People in the other boxes turned toward them and scowled. She regained her composure and, for the first time, looked directly at Donovan. Her makeup was smeared, and age lines showed on her face. She was not so pretty now.

"This was his reaction. You are looking at his reaction. When you look at me right now, and I see the expression on your face, the shock you cannot hide when you look at me, you are looking at Samuel's face that night. What he looked like that night. And he looked like every night of his life since. Until they murdered him."

"Who murdered him?"

"Who do you think? I will not say the words for you. God is not going to judge me for what I did or didn't do that night. You are not the instrument of God that you pretend to be. Now go. Security is very tight here. We live well, but lots of bad things can happen to people like me in Mexico, and they keep a careful eye on us to see no one disturbs us, disturbs our lives. Go. Leave me alone. Go back to Sanasauk."

CHAPTER 9

The Ways and Means Committee of Sanasauk City Council consisted of four Democrats and three Republicans. But when it came to cop issues, party designation was irrelevant. What mattered was that the Police Federation had endorsed three members of the committee in the last election. The other four had defeated the Fed candidates.

"So, Officer Moore," said Peter Moe, the committee chair, "as I understand it, these are your demands on behalf of the Federation: a six percent across-the-board increase, and we add Arbor Day and Columbus Day to the official holiday list for double-time pay.

"Let me ask you, can we assume that the Italian Americans on the force are also tree huggers, so maybe we could get by on just one holiday?"

"Chairman Moe, you may think this stuff is funny, but the men are at the lowest point in their morale which I have ever seen them at," said Dinty Moore. "This is very, very serious. I come to you in all my seriousness representing all the men and women who risk their lives every day on behalf of the citizens of this community and ask only fairness in return. Fairness, that's all we ask."

"Okay, Officer Moore. Fairness. Fairness means fairness to all, doesn't it?" said Moe. He didn't wait for an answer. "The police payroll runs about $40,000 per officer. Take that times 1,200 officers. That's $48,000,000. So if we grant the police request for a six percent increase, we'll have to fund an additional $2,800,000. That's just for the police. To say nothing of the firefighters and the rest of the city employees who want to tailgate on any increase we give you.

"We don't have it. We'll have to raise property taxes. Every homeowner in Sanasauk will have to pay an average of about $75 more in property taxes next year to pay for your increase. As you say, Officer Moore, fairness. We're talking about fairness here. Seventy-five dollars may not sound like much to you, but we've got a lot of folks on fixed incomes here. Folks who have to skip meals or not take their medicines to scrape up another $75 for you.

"Fairness. Be nice if we could pay for your demand out of a surplus, but we don't have a surplus anymore. We are running a budget deficit this year of about $3 million, which will wipe out our surplus. In fairness—and I have to be fair—I must tell you that the major part of that deficit is the result of things over which we had no control, like the worst snowfall in the city's history, so we're forty percent overbudget for snow removal. Then, we had a breakdown at the water plant, causing our water supply to be interrupted for three days, involving emergency repairs.

"But here's the item I want to call to your special attention: $760,000 representing out-of-court settlements in four cases involving police misconduct. Four cases. Let me review these cases: One, Sergeant—a sergeant, mind you—Henry Hightower and his partner, Officer Gerald Ickes, arrest two Native American citizens for D and D. Rather than transporting them in the back of their black-and-white, the officers tell them they smell so bad they'll have to ride in the trunk, so they make them climb in, they shut the trunk lid, and that's where they take the ride downtown. Cost to the city: $250,000 plus legal fees. Very expensive ride. Maybe they should have called a cab.

"Two, Officer William Pearson, while on routine patrol, runs over the foot of a pedestrian with his squad car. Officer Pearson squeaks by the breath test by one-tenth of a percent, but nonetheless, cost to the city: $60,000.

"Three, Officer Amelia Sanchez, while arresting and handcuffing a demonstrator at a Fight the Fur Freaks rally, breaks the wrist of one Mrs. Arthur Wright Parker Jr., who happens to be a sixty-five-year-old lady of some repute in this town. Cost to city: $175,000 plus a written apology from Officer Sanchez, the mayor, the chief, and a resolution of apology from the Sanasauk City Council, signed by all members of this committee, including yours truly. Incidentally, Mrs. Wright Parker Jr. donated her settlement to charity, half to Fight the Fur Freaks, and the other half—that's $137,500, Officer Moore— to a new organization, MOP. MOP, Monitor Our Police, for which organization, Mrs. Wright Parker has agreed to serve as president and principal fundraiser. I'm sure we'll be hearing more from them as time goes by.

"Four, Sergeant Manfred DePuy—another sergeant, mind you—Officers Harold Grimes, Walter Peterson, Dudley Granger, Nathan Holmes, and Officer Dennis Moore—that's you, I believe— while raiding what they think is a crack house, break into, and I mean break, at three a.m., the homestead of one George and Wilma Davis, their three sons, George Junior, Darius, and Tyler, and their daughter, Desiree, rousting out and generally messing up said home- stead before discovering that they have the wrong address. Cost to city: $275,000 plus written apologies from said officers, the chief, the mayor, and a resolution from us.

"Now, Officer Moore, Federation President Moore, thank you for your input on this fine day. We will take your demands under advisement here...I see Officer Moore is leaving us, no doubt to resume his raiding duties...so for those of you in attendance who take a continuing interest in these proceedings, let me remind you we meet again in three weeks. If there are no objections, this meeting is adjourned."

Two days later, ten percent of the Sanasauk called in sick. Within a week, blue flu had struck twenty-five percent of the Sanasauk police department. That afternoon, four people met in the mayor's office: Mayor Sensaboe, District Attorney Barlow, Chief of Police Reagan, and Council President Moe.

"All right, Mr. Barlow, where do we stand legally? Do I have to call it an illegal strike before I ask the governor to call out the National Guard?" said Sensaboe.

"No. All you have to do is provide him with a legitimate reason. It's enough that you have determined that there is a threat to the public safety. It's up to him to agree with you or not," said Barlow.

"What do you think, Peter? Will they meet with you? Can we get some negotiations going at least?"

"Why don't you call a spade a spade, Mr. Mayor?" said Moe. "They're breaking the law. They gave up the right to strike when they took the King's shilling. Why are you letting them get away with it? They're trying to blackmail us into a settlement we can't afford and the people don't want."

"Chief, what do the numbers show? Any increase in incidents since this started?"

"You mean the overnights? No, nothing special. The usual amount of the bread-and-butter stuff, burglaries, auto thefts, etc."

"Do you expect that to change?"

"No. One of two of our more adventurous adversaries may test the waters, but we're not really being stretched at this point. Frankly, along with most other urban police departments, we're overstaffed by about the same number now taking to their beds."

"Not exactly taking to their beds, Chief. Take a peek out the window. They're walking around in front waving their signs," said the mayor. "Peter, why don't you go back to the table with them?"

"I can't do that, sir, unless I have something to offer them? What do you suggest?" said Moe.

"Mr. Mayor, may I make a comment?" said Reagan. "They have two weeks sick leave, so after another week or so, they won't be drawing any salary, and the Fed strike fund won't carry them more than a week or so after that. From then on, they'll be on their own. No paycheck. And ninety-nine percent of them don't have a nickel saved. The wife is going to be waving the bills around and asking how they're going to pay little Jimmy's orthodontist.

"The ones you got out there now are all they're going to get, and the longer it lasts, the more of those will be going to go back to work. The papers won't play this big because even though the editorial writers are bleeding hearts, that applies to minorities and women, not to cops, especially on labor issues. The owners know the *Newspaper Guild* will use a favorable settlement on our part to up their demands. We'll have to give them something, but we don't have to knuckle under."

"You remind me of one of the kind of liberals Gene McCarthy used to talk about. They'd see you drowning twenty feet offshore, throw you a rope ten feet long, and say they've met you halfway."

"Give it some time, Mr. Mayor," said the chief. "It'll calm down."

"Will it?" said the mayor. "Do you hear what they're shouting out there?"

"No," said the chief.

The mayor went over to the window and threw it open.

"Eddie. Eddie. Eddie."

"Gentlemen, thank you for your input. Chief, stick around. I want to have a word with you," said the mayor.

The others left.

"Chief," said the mayor. "I welcome your advice, but not your timing. I don't need Moe and Barlow to hear you tell me how I should be handling this. A year from now either one could be running against me. My questions were quite specific. Keep your counsel on policy matters between us."

"Yes, sir."

"That'll be all."

CHAPTER 10

It wasn't the women, though she supposed there had been some. A vice squad is like a professional ball club. Ballplayers get so many offers they're considered paragons of morality if they take the freebies just when they're on the road. Jim Bouton, the author of the first tell-all sports book, recalled when he was playing in Triple A, just one rung below the majors. Holding his index finger and his thumb a hair apart, the manager, Charlie Dressen, told the team, "Remember, guys, you're only this far from major league pussy." Bouton wrote that it was the most inspirational pep talk he ever heard as a professional ballplayer. No, thought Emily Steinmetz, it wasn't the women. It was the drinking, the drinking that grew steadily worse, and the black moods that went with it.

She had wanted to be more than the typical nagging wife. She had tried to distract him, to show him there was something more to life than the cop's bleak view of the human condition.

Once she had organized a theater outing. Five couples. Wining and dining at one of the best restaurants in Sanasauk. She had spent a fortune on her dress, her own money, and the better part of a day getting ready. The play was *The House of Atreus*, a Greek tragedy performed en masque, everyone in togas and a chanting chorus mounted on tiers at the sides of the stage. He walked out at the end of the first act. "I'm leaving *The House of Atreus*," he said. "And don't expect me tonight at the House of Steinmetz."

Perhaps it had been a bit pretentious.

Finally, he had been the one to move out. A note on the refrigerator door. His clothes gone, but everything else, the record collection, the pictures, except for a couple of Katie, all left behind. She was glad he still wanted to be a good father, and he was, pretty much. He took Katie most weekends, even attended a few parent-teacher conferences. But when she tried to find out from Katie what his private life had become, she could tell her mother very little. Katie had never seen his apartment, nor had he ever spoken of another woman. And of course, he never had so much as a sip of anything alcoholic around his daughter, so she couldn't tell if he was still drinking heavily.

She knew she would have to call him as a witness, and she dreaded it, but it was the job, and the job had become her life, such as it was.

The case was to be tried before Judge Howard Gunderson, who, like most judges, had been appointed to the bench because he was a lawyer who knew a governor. As State Senator Howard Gunderson, he had supported the governor's legislative program with more loyalty than necessary from a purely personal standpoint, earning himself an early retirement from the rough and tumble of elective politics.

Looking up at him from below his judicial perch, he appeared to be a large man. But when he stepped down from the dais to the level occupied by ordinary mortals, it became apparent that only his head and his voice were large. Like many a former legislative water boy, once he had his own show, he ran it with an iron fist. Judge Gunderson did not suffer fools gladly.

Eddie White had made a shrewd choice for a cop charged with murdering two blacks. Peerless Jackson was the best black criminal lawyer in Sanasauk, and possibly the best, period. Sweet natured, bow-tied, rotund, deferential, but never Uncle Tomish—a winning quality when appearing before the imperious Gunderson—he was an effective pleader with a laser-like ability to focus on the one juror he needed to hold out for an acquittal. The mantra among the most affluent and the most guilty was, "You better be fearless, or you better get Peerless."

The trial got underway with Judge Gunderson telling a Kenneth Starr joke in the course of explaining the awesome responsibilities of a juror to the panel. While the lawyers were compelled to laugh at any attempt at judicial humor, however feeble or inappropriate, they also observed the jury panel closely. Two prospective jurors joined in the fun.

Peerless marked his chart.

He'd take a bleeding heart or two, based on his observation that liberals seemed to have trouble convicting anyone of anything, even a cop killing a couple of black cop killers. But he definitely wanted no blacks. He could already feel waves of hostility sweeping over him from the blacks on the jury panel. He knew that in their eyes, he might as well be defending Mark Furhman. He scanned the list for suburbanites who had fled the inner city, middle-income Republicans, nervous housewives, retirees on fixed incomes, union members, regular churchgoers, particularly Fundies and Catholics. What he wouldn't give to be a fly on the wall in the jury room during deliberations when the blue-collar whites and the blacks got into it. Emily's take on the joke had been to mark the two laughers as keepers, on the theory that anti-Starrs would be less sympathetic to cops. Her wish list tilted toward upper-income types, college graduates, Jews, Unitarians, and other liberal Protestants, fallen-away Catholics, academics, civil servants, inner-city residents, and especially blacks.

Voir dire took all day. By the time it was over, the usual mix emerged. Both sides had five they liked, five they didn't, and two they were unsure of.

The actual trial began the next day. Opening arguments were bombastic and unrevealing of the evidence that would be presented.

"Ms. Steinmetz, call your first witness," said Judge Gunderson.

She called Howard Jamison, the medical examiner, who described the nature of Witherspoon's wounds and the cause of death.

"Dr. Jamison, what was the level of alcohol in the victim's body?"

"Point zero six."

"What would that correspond to for a man of Mr. Witherspoon's size and weight in terms of number of drinks he'd consumed?"

"About two ounces of 86 proof whiskey."

"Is that enough to make him intoxicated?"

"Depends on the individual. But from this man's size and weight, I'd say no."

"Dr. Jamison, did you weigh the victim's body?"

"What we had to work with, yes."

"What did the victim weigh?"

"In pounds, two hundred and thirty pounds, eleven ounces."

"Would you estimate as his true total weight at the time of death?"

"I estimate two hundred and thirty-eight pounds, eleven ounces."

"How did you arrive at that estimate?"

"The average human head weighs twenty-two pounds. Mr. Witherspoon had a large head. I'd estimate it weighed twenty-four pounds. Approximately one-third of Mr. Witherspoon's head was missing when we examined his body."

"And Dr. Jamison, what was the victim wearing at the time of his death?"

"Boxer shorts, undershirt, socks, a watch."

"Is it customary for people to wander around outside in thirty-degree weather in their underwear?"

"Objection. Foundation."

"Sustained. Jury will disregard. Continue, Counsel."

"And, Dr. Jamison, were there any traces of residue from gunfire on the victim's hands?"

"No."

"Any other foreign substance on the victim's body?"

"Yes."

"What?"

"Shards of glass on the shoulders and what remained of the head."

"Were you able to identify the shards of glass?"

"Yes."

"Please describe your findings."

"The glass—I recovered eighteen pieces—all less than one millimeter long, very thin, frosted, several pieces curved. I sent a couple of pieces off to the FBI boys in Washington. They said in their report that they were from a shattered one-hundred-watt GE lightbulb. Pretty standard item."

"Do you have that report with you today?"

"Yes."

"Your Honor, we'd like to have this marked and entered into evidence as state's exhibit number 9."

"Has Defendant had a chance to examine it?"

"Counsel is examining it now, Your Honor," said Emily.

"Any objections?"

"No objections, Your Honor," said Peerless.

"Received. Mark it as state's exhibit number 9," said Gunderson. Emily continued.

"Is there any way to determine how that shattered glass came to be on the victim's body?"

"Yes."

"What would that be?"

"If there was a lightbulb directly above him that was shattered by the same blast that killed him."

"Thank you, Dr. Jamison. That will be all I have for now."

"Mr. Jackson, cross-examination?" said Judge Gunderson.

"Yes, sir."

"About the drinks, Dr. Jamison. Was it possible he could have consumed more than two ounces of whiskey if he'd taken the drinks more than, say, an hour before his death?"

"Yes, it's possible."

"Considerably more?"

"All depends on when he drank them."

"Yes. Dr. Jamison, you said there was no gunfire residue on the victim's hands, but isn't it possible he still may have fired a handgun, and the residue was dissipated by the hands having been submerged in a melting pile of snow before the body was removed?"

"It's possible."

"So you cannot be sure he did not fire a gun immediately prior to Officer White's returning fire, can you?"

"Objection. Assuming a fact not in evidence. We have no evidence Officer White was returning anyone's fire here."

"Sustained. Rephrase your question, Counsel."

"Dr. Jamison, based on your examination, you cannot be sure that Samuel Witherspoon did not fire a gun immediately prior to his death, can you?"

"No, sir."

"Thank you. That's all."

"Your Honor, the state calls Gloria Two Bears."

Gloria was sworn in and asked what she did for a living. She said she was a waitress at The Lodge. The Lodge is a shithole, but if you happen to live in Sanasauk and are of the Native American persuasion, it's about all you have in the way of a place of respite from the cares of the day. Gloria Two Bears spent almost every evening at The Lodge, but not to drink. Gloria was a teetotaler and proud of it.

"Ms. Two Bears, isn't it also a fact that you work as a prostitute out of The Lodge?"

"Your Honor, Counsel is impeaching her own witness," said Peerless, rising.

"Your Honor," said Steinmetz, "I could have called Ms. Two Bears as a hostile witness under the rules, and I will if I have to, but until she indicates otherwise, I would like to treat her as a state's witness."

"Mr. Jackson, you will object now or forever hold your peace. Once we get going, you've waived on that grounds."

"No objection, Your Honor. We'll let 'er ride."

"Ms. Two Bears, please describe your relationship to the victim, Samuel Witherspoon."

Two Bears rambled through her long, sometimes professional, sometimes consensual, sometimes loving, sometimes violent relationship with Samuel Witherspoon.

"Tell us what happened the night Samuel Witherspoon was killed."

"He was in The Lodge, drinking. He motions me to come over. We talk for a while. He say he wants to go back to my place. I say okay. When we get there, I tell him it's the end of the month, and I need money for rent. He says, 'Let's do it first.' I say I need the money first. We get into an argument, and he starts hitting me. I hit him back. He's real drunk too. Next thing I know, I hear somebody call him. He goes outside. Then bang, bang, bang. Lots of noise. Bust the light. He goes over the rail. That's all I know. Police all over the place. Big mess. He bust the rail too."

"Ms. Two Bears, you say you heard someone call him. How did they call him?"

"I dunno."

"Do you know if they called his name?"

"Objection. Repetitive. Witness said she didn't know."

"Your Honor, I'm just trying to refresh her recollection."

"Overruled. You may answer, witness."

"Maybe. They could have called his name. I dunno. I'm not sure what they called."

"They? Was there more than one."

"No. I don't think so."

"Was he called more than once?"

"Yes. I think they called a couple times."

"You keep saying 'they'?"

"No, just one calling. That's just the way I talk."

"What was he wearing?"

"Underpants. He strips down soon as he comes over. He don't like to waste time."

The jurors laughed. The judge gavelled them into silence. Only one comedian allowed in this courtroom.

"Did you see a gun in his hand?"

"No."

"At any time that evening, did you see him in possession of a firearm?"

"No."

"At the time he went out, was the door from your apartment to the porch open?"

"Maybe a little. It gets real hot in my place."

Laughter. Gavel.

"Were you going to have—strike that, were you going to engage in relations with the victim with the door to your apartment open, anyone could walk in?"

"I told you, I'm not going to do anything unless Samuel gives me some money."

"If he had given you the money, would you have left the door open?"

"Objection. Speculative."

"Sustained. Counsel will rephrase."

"Are you in the habit of having sexual relations with your outside door open so anyone could walk right in?"

"Sometimes. Sure."

The jury laughed again. Gunderson gavelled furiously.

"Ms. Two Bears, was the porch light on when the victim went out on the porch?"

"I don't know."

"Was it on when you came home with him?"

"I think so."

"Could it have been off?"

"Yes, it could have."

"So you're not sure, are you?"

"Objection, repetitive. She's asked the same question three times."

"And gotten three different answers, Your Honor."

"Overruled. Continue. Reread the question."

The clerk reread the question, "'So you're not sure, are you?'"

"No, I am not sure."

"Ms. Two Bears, do you recognize the defendant?"

"Sure. Sergeant White."

"How do you happen to know him?"

"He arrested me."

Laughter. Gavelling.

"What did he arrest you for?"

"Prostitution."

"Are you a prostitute?"

"Sometimes I have to do things I don't like to do. Money is hard to come by for Indian people in Sanasauk."

"How many times did Sergeant White arrest you?"

"Once."

"When was that?"

"Couple years ago."

"More like a year and a half ago, wasn't it?"

"Could be."

"How many times prior to that had you been arrested for prostitution?"

"I don't know?"

Emily walked back to the prosecutors' table and picked up a document.

"Do you dispute that you have been arrested for prostitution eleven times?"

"That sounds okay."

"Your Honor, we would ask to place in evidence this document, the arrest record of Gloria Two Bears as state's exhibit number twelve? Copy to defense counsel."

"Any objections?"

Peerless shook his head.

"Received."

"How many times have you been arrested for prostitution subsequent to the time you were arrested by Defendant?"

"I don't remember."

"You don't remember that you have not been arrested since Defendant arrested you? You do not remember that you have not been arrested for prostitution, or for anything else, in the last year and a half, even though in a seven-year period of time prior to that you were arrested eleven times?"

"I don't remember."

"You don't remember. But you remember Defendant all right. Okay, Ms. Two Bears, do you remember making a deal with Defendant?"

"No."

"Do you remember Defendant telling you that he had done you a favor and that you owed him one?"

"No."

"Do you remember Defendant telling you he wanted you to tell him when Samuel Witherspoon came over?"

"No."

"Do you remember calling Defendant the evening Samuel Witherspoon was killed and telling him Samuel Witherspoon was in The Lodge and might be coming over to see you?"

"No. How could I call him? He was in a police car."

"I'll ask the questions here, Ms. Two Bears, but this time I'll answer yours. Because even though he was in a police car, he was carrying his own private cell phone, that's how."

"Objection. Who's testifying here, Counsel or the witness? Move to strike."

"Sustained. Jury will disregard."

"Defendant gave you his cell phone number to call, didn't he?"

"No."

"Do you deny you placed a call to him from The Lodge on the night Samuel Witherspoon was murdered?"

"Objection to the word *murder*."

"Sustained. Counsel, you're getting carried away here."

"I apologize, Your Honor. On the night Samuel Witherspoon died with his head blown off by a shotgun blast from Defendant."

"Objection. Inflammatory."

"Sustained. Counsel, I told you to phrase your questions in the proper manner. You are bordering on contempt here."

"Yes, Your Honor. I apologize to the court and to the witness. Ms. Two Bears, do you deny placing a call from The Lodge to Defendant on his cell phone on the night Samuel Witherspoon was killed?"

"I deny it."

Emily went back to the table and returned with a sheet of paper she handed to Gloria Two Bears.

"Please tell the jury what you are holding in your hand."

"A piece of paper from the phone company."

"What does it say?"

"It says there was a phone call that night from 374-1215 to 922-8264 at 11:12 p.m."

"Can you identify those phone numbers?"

"No."

"Look at the piece of paper again."

"I'm looking."

"Isn't it a fact that one of those phone numbers is the pay phone at The Lodge, and the other phone number is Defendant's cell phone."

"It says at the top of the paper that the cell phone number belongs to Sergeant White. But it doesn't say that the other number is from The Lodge."

"Okay, Ms. Two Bears, we'll have someone verify that later. Your Honor, we would like to place this document in evidence—my colleague is handing a copy to defense counsel—state's exhibit number thirteen."

"Any objections? Received."

"Your Honor, I have no further questions at this time."

"Mr. Jackson?"

"Thank you, Your Honor."

"Ms. Two Bears, are you employed?"

"Yes, I work at The Lodge."

"Doing what?"

"I am a waitress."

"How long have you been employed there?"

"About two years. No, about a year and a half."

"Your Honor, we would like to place in evidence Ms. Two Bear's W-2s and time sheets from The Lodge over the last two years and have them marked as Defendant's exhibit number four."

"Any objections? Received."

"What did you do prior to that time?"

"I prostituted myself."

"What made you become a waitress?"

"I got tired of being arrested. I was disgusted with myself. I wanted to do something better, something so I wouldn't feel so bad all the time."

"So you became a waitress."

"Yes."

"Did you still prostitute yourself?"

"Sometimes. Sometimes I had to. Like with Samuel. And when I needed money real bad. But no, not on a regular basis. I quit doing that after Sergeant White arrested me."

"Did Sergeant White say anything to you to encourage you to quit?"

"Kind of."

"What did he say?"

"He said it would go hard on me if he had to arrest me again."

"What do you think he meant by that?"

"I don't know."

"Do you think he meant that he might use physical violence on you?"

"Maybe, I don't know."

"Did you have any sort of deal with Sergeant White?"

"No. I did not want to have anything to do with him."

"Why?"

"He frightened me."

"So you did not call him the night Witherspoon was killed?"

"No. Someone else must have called him. He had lots of people."

"You mean he had people they call snitches?"

"Yes."

"Why would a snitch call him?"

"Someone doing something there. Like drugs. Or prostituting themselves."

"Was anyone prostituting themselves at The Lodge or doing drugs that night?"

"They do that in there every night."

"Every night?"

"Every night I ever been there."

"Ms. Two Bears, did you ever see Mr. Witherspoon with a gun?"

"Sure. He used to be a cop. He always had a gun."

"Ms. Two Bears, you testified earlier that when Mr. Witherspoon went out on the porch, you heard a 'bang, bang, bang.' That's three bangs, am I correct? You heard three bangs."

"Three bangs."

"Not one bang. Not two bangs. Three bangs?"

"Three bangs."

"Thank you. That's all I have, Your Honor."

"Any further questions, Ms. Steinmetz?"

"Yes, just a few. These bangs you said you heard, can you identify them, Ms. Two Bears?"

"Identify them?"

"What they were. Could you tell what they were?"

"One sounded like a shotgun. Pow. It made a big noise."

"What about the other two?"

"Could have been a gun."

"Could it also have been a car door slamming? Your porch door slamming?"

"Could have been."

"That's all I have at this time, Your Honor."

"Mr. Jackson?"

"Which came first, Ms. Two Bears, the big bang or the other bangs?"

"I don't remember."

"Could the other bangs have come first?"

"They could have."

"No further questions."

"Ms. Steinmetz?"

"Just one, Your Honor. Ms. Two Bears, so the noise, which could possibly have been door slams could have come prior to the big bang you identified as the shotgun blast, am I right?"

"Yes."

"That's all I have at this time, Your Honor."

"Mr. Jackson?"

"Nothing more at this time, Your Honor."

"You may step down, Ms. Two Bears. You are dismissed, subject to recall."

Court adjourned for the day.

CHAPTER 11

Emily was totally drained. By the time she got home, Katie had already fixed her own dinner and gone to bed. She had left a note on the refrigerator saying she had gotten an A+ on her history paper and that she knew Mom was working hard and was real busy and hoped Mom had had a good day too. Emily wondered whether Katie knew that she was going to have to call her dad as a witness. Probably. Katie was only eleven, but not much got by her.

Emily felt she had gotten most of what she had wanted from Jamison and Two Bears. She had thought about saving the cell phone for Ed White, but he was sure to be ready for it. Gloria had been surprised, and she doubted that the jury bought the business about someone else making the call.

She turned on the eleven o'clock news. They led off with the police strike and then segued into the trial. She thought it was dumb for the cops to tie their cause to a thug like Ed White. But that's cops for you. That secret-society-circle-the-wagons attitude was why they were in that courtroom in the first place—and why she was no longer married to a cop.

*****

"Counsel, call your next witness."

"The state calls Dr. Irving Horowitz."

Horowitz was a psychiatrist who served as a consultant to the Sanasauk PD. He had examined Witherspoon in connection with

83

the hearing at the time of Witherspoon's suspension and subsequent discharge from the police force.

"And what were your findings, Doctor?"

"Severe depression."

"Symptoms?"

"This was a man who several years earlier had been something of a fitness fanatic, a participant in various community outreach and police-sponsored athletic events, a speaker at schools and churches on behalf of moral values, good nutrition, physical conditioning, continuing education, a role model, actually, particularly for inner-city kids.

"At the time of my examination, he was forty pounds over-weight, drinking heavily, lethargic, unresponsive, disengaged, bor-derline hallucinatory, borderline paranoic—in layman's terms, a mental basket case."

"Cause?"

"Any number of possibilities. Physical decline. The pressure of the work. Triggering incident."

"You said 'paranoic.' Who did he think was after him?"

"I said 'borderline paranoic.' Who was after him? Everyone. Fellow officers, neighbors, relatives, the newspaper boy who couldn't seem to get the paper all the way up to the front door and left it by his garage every morning. Part of a conspiracy to prevent him from learning what was going on in the world. Everyone."

"During your examination, did he mention a specific triggering incident?"

"Yes."

"What did he say?"

"He said that one of the principal reasons he had become a policeman was because African Americans shouldn't always have to deal with white people as policemen but that it hadn't done any good, that he had been a failure."

"The specific incident, what did he say about that?"

"That there had been a time when the chips were down, and he'd had a chance to do the right thing, and he had been a coward.

That he had been afraid to act and as a result let everyone down, including himself."

"That's it?"

"That's it."

"Did you know what he was talking about?"

"I had an idea, but my role was not investigative. It was to evaluate his fitness to continue as a police officer, and in my opinion, there were too many demons. He couldn't handle it."

"What was your idea?"

"Objection. Speculative. Anyone can make guesses. I'm sure Dr. Horowitz reads the same newspapers we all do."

"I'm asking for a professional opinion here, Your Honor, not a guess."

"Objection sustained. We're too far afield from an expert opinion here, Counsel."

"Dr. Horowitz, is it your expert opinion that Samuel Witherspoon was a deeply troubled, deeply disturbed man and that the cause of that disturbance may have been an incident involving police work with particular reference to African Americans?"

"Yes."

"Thank you. Your witness."

"Dr. Horowitz, in your expert opinion, could the cause of Samuel Witherspoon's depression have been a personal incident, such as a failed romance?"

"Well, it could have been."

"So your answer is yes."

"My answer is it could have been."

"No further questions."

"Call your next witness, Ms. Steinmetz."

"The state calls John Steinmetz."

He was in his dress blues, of course. Cops always get spiffed up for their courtroom appearances. It makes a hell of an impression on a jury. Gleaming metal flashed from the bars on his collar and his badge and name bar, but not from a gun. Witnesses, even cops, are not allowed to have guns in the courtroom.

"Lieutenant Steinmetz, just so the jury doesn't get confused, please indicate the nature of our relationship." She wanted the jury to know she wasn't hiding anything from them, even though the press had been full of it, and she was sure they already knew.

"Okay. We're divorced. Two and a half years now. We're parents of a child. She's eleven now. We share custody."

"Thank you. Now, Lieutenant, please describe your actions on the night in question here." Steinmetz went into the usual robotic drone that policemen affect when they're testifying, referring occasionally to the piece of paper he held in his left hand for sticky details like exact times. Standing at her counsel table, Emily glanced down at her copy of the same document. It was the official report he had filed the night of the incident.

He finished.

"Did you touch or handle any of the firearms involved in the incident?"

"I had Sergeant White give me his handgun, but otherwise, no."

"You didn't handle or touch the shotgun that Defendant used?"

"No."

"What about the piece that the victim allegedly fired?"

"I didn't touch it. Neither did Olson. We left it for Homicide."

"Did you disturb the body of the victim in any way prior to the arrival of the medical examiner?"

"No, but my partner, Harlan Olson, checked the pockets for ID. That's when I found out it was Witherspoon."

"Did you know who it was prior to that?"

"No."

"Did Defendant give any indication he knew who it was prior to that?"

"No."

"Did he tell you what happened?"

"Yeah."

"What did he say?"

"Objection. Hearsay."

"Your Honor, he's testifying as to the report, which is in evidence."

"Overruled. Continue."

"Well, it's in the report, so I can't add too much. He was kind of shook up, of course. He said he heard the arguing and sounds like they were really going at it, so he pulled in and started to get out of the car when this guy steps out on the porch with a gun and starts waving it around. He ducks back in the car and pulls out the shotgun. He identifies himself, tells the guy to drop it, and the guy takes a couple shots at him, so he returns fire. That's about it."

"Did he say whether he called him out?"

"No."

"Did he say whether the porch light was on?"

"Yeah, he said the light was off."

"Did you hear any shots fired?"

"No."

"How soon after the incident occurred did you arrive on the scene?"

"We were there three minutes after we got the call for backup."

"How do you account for the rapid response?"

"We usually have to account for an unrapid response." There was a titter in the courtroom that died before Gunderson could swing his gavel. "But we were just fortunate to be in the area. This is a high-crime area. We do a lot of patrolling there."

"So you and Sergeant White were both patrolling the same area, right?"

"Right."

"Had you seen Sergeant White earlier in the evening?"

"Yeah."

"How soon before the incident?"

"Half an hour or so."

"Did you talk to him?"

"Yeah. Rolled down the windows. 'How's it going? Let's hope it's a quiet one.' That sort of thing. Talked maybe a minute or so."

"You were driving the squad that you and Officer Olson were patrolling in?"

"Yeah."

"Isn't it unusual for a lieutenant to be driving a patrolman around?"

"Not really. He'd been on foot patrol downtown for a couple of years. He didn't know the area as well as me, so I was kind of showing him the ropes, drop by the hot spots so he could see what they looked like. Besides, I don't like the way anyone drives as well as the way I drive. I'd rather drive. I'm more relaxed when I'm doing the driving."

"How well do you know Sergeant White?"

"Pretty well."

"Have you ever been involved in other shooting incidents with him?"

"Involved? I suppose you could say that."

"One very notorious incident, if I'm not mistaken, am I not?"

"Objection. This is irrelevant."

"Your Honor, may we approach?" said Emily.

"Yes. Clerk, sidebar."

The judge leaned over to hear the two lawyers, who had gathered with the court stenographer at the side of the bench away from the jury. Peerless got in the first lick.

"Your Honor," said Peerless, "she is going to try to smear my client by suggesting that he and the witness conspired to murder Witherspoon because of some ancient grudge, something to do with their both being present when Sergeant White took down two cop killers. This is ridiculous. This is outrageous. That incident was thoroughly investigated by the department, and my client even got a promotion as a result of his heroism there."

"Steinmetz?" said Judge Gunderson.

"Your Honor, we have ample evidence to support our charge that Sergeant White did this murder. We are going to present that evidence. But I need to establish the motive. That's why I need to explore this prior incident. Witherspoon was going to blow the whistle on this so-called heroism. The shooting of Witherspoon is the conclusion of a continuing event that began with that earlier shooting."

"Steinmetz, I will allow you to pursue this on condition that you can tie this to what we're dealing with here. If it becomes apparent you cannot, I will strike the testimony. Jackson, your motion is denied, but I will grant a motion for you to strike the word *notorious*. Nothing has been proven, not yet anyway, to permit the use of that word."

"I so move, Your Honor. Exception to the ruling on the earlier shooting."

"Exception noted. Continue."

Emily went through the killing of the Hope murder suspects. Her questions told the story she wanted to sell to the jury. Witherspoon had caught up with the suspects and was holding them at gunpoint when the other three cops arrived. Instead of placing them under arrest, White killed them in cold blood. Witherspoon, watching in horror while two defenseless black teenagers were shot dead as he stood by helplessly, had gone into a downward spiral from which he never recovered.

As the ranking officer present when the shootings occurred, Steinmetz bore a share of the responsibility. As the ranking officer and a participant, if not the planner and instigator of the coverup, Steinmetz was an accomplice after the fact to murder.

"And, Lieutenant, you also deny having any foreknowledge that Sergeant White planned to carry out the murder of Samuel Witherspoon?"

"Yes. Definitely. I totally deny it."

"Lieutenant, I am sure Counsel for Defendant will be sharing with the jury your outstanding record as a member of the Sanasauk Police Department, but before he gets into that, I have one further area I wish to explore with you. Are you a drinker?"

"A drinker? Do you mean do I take a drink every now and then?"

"I mean has your drinking ever gotten you in trouble?"

"With you, it has." There was a buzz. Gunderson quickly gavelled the courtroom into silence. "But if you mean legal trouble, yeah, once, before I was even on the force, I got a DUI."

"Since then?"

"I've never had a problem."

"Had you had anything alcoholic to drink the night the two suspects were killed by Officer White?"

"Sergeant White? No."

"He was Officer White then, but no matter. Your testimony is that you had nothing to drink that night, correct?"

"That's what I said."

"No further questions at this time. Your witness, Mr. Jackson."

Emily had conducted most of her examination from behind counsel's table, as far as she could get from her ex-husband. Peerless did the reverse, getting so close to Steinmetz as to practically jump into the witness box with him.

"Lieutenant, we are going to tell the jury about your career on the Sanasauk Police Department. Is that agreeable?" Jackson began.

He went over Steinmetz's record, the fitness reports, the citations, the arrest record, the promotions, the advanced schooling in police work paid for by the city.

"Are you an active member of the Police Federation, Lieutenant?"

"Yes."

"Is Sergeant White also active in the Federation?"

"Very active. He's a board member."

"The Police Federation is currently in a rather heated dispute with the city and the administration of the department, aren't they?"

"Yes."

"Do you think that has anything to do with the reason why we are here today?"

"Objection. Speculative."

"Approach, Your Honor?" said Jackson.

"All right. Clerk," said Judge Gunderson.

The lawyers and the stenographer huddled beside the bench.

"Your Honor, this is just payback for your earlier ruling. This is beyond speculation. It's fantasy," said Emily.

"Your Honor, if the state can make up motives out of whole cloth, we should be able to have opinions on that subject too," said Jackson.

"You have a point, Counsel, but let's not take this too far. Overruled."

Peerless didn't really expect anyone on the jury to buy his theory. But he knew when they went at it during the deliberations, jurors leaning toward his client would need a tool to blunt the more plausible motive Emily had brought out.

"Lieutenant, state's attorney has brought up an incident that occurred many years ago in order to establish a motive for my client to have deliberately taken Samuel Witherspoon's life. Your Honor, we have furnished a copy of the Sanasauk Police Department's official report on this incident to state's attorney, and we would now like to have it marked and placed in evidence as Defendant's exhibit number five."

"No objections."

"Received. Mark it, please."

"Lieutenant, I am handing you Defendant's exhibit number five, and I'm going to refer to various parts of this document and ask you to read from it."

Peerless went through the IA version of the Hope murder and the Hoover/Payne shootings at length.

"Lieutenant, I will now refer you to the conclusion of the report dealing with the conduct of the police officers involved."

As Steinmetz read the leaden bureaucratic prose studded with nuggets like "risk of his own life," "fulfillment of their sworn duty," "best traditions of the Sanasauk Police Department," "commended," and "acted with merit," Emily saw Jackson, White, and her ex-husband sneaking sly glances at her for signs of despair.

CHAPTER 12

"The state calls the defendant, Edward White, for cross-examination under the rules."

Eddie White was the only person she knew of who managed to lumber and swagger at the same time. *It must be a cop thing,* she thought.

He was big in every way. Big body, big voice, big head of wavy blond hair, handsome in a florid way. There was no mistaking him for anything but what he was, a street cop.

Emily went through the preliminaries and then moved on to the cornfield shootings, setting up her motive hypothesis again with a series of questions which White answered by referring to the IA report and denying any wrongdoing.

"So that if Samuel Witherspoon or anyone present that night were to claim they saw you deliberately shoot Stephen Hoover and Marvin Payne after they had been disarmed, subdued, and were being held at gunpoint, they would be lying, am I correct?"

"Yes."

"And you had no reason to silence Samuel Witherspoon forever by taking his life, am I correct?"

"Yes. I liked Sam. I felt bad he got bounced. I felt even worse about the shooting."

"And you were not aware at the time that the person whom you killed four years later was Samuel Witherspoon, right?"

"Right."

"All right, Sergeant White. We're now going to go over the killing of Samuel Witherspoon. Before we get started, let me ask, have you rehearsed your testimony with your counsel?"

"No. I discussed it. I didn't rehearse it."

As Emily expected, White claimed the phone call from The Lodge had come from one of his snitches, Leon Beauchamp, now conveniently deceased.

"Where were you when you first heard the discussion taking place between Samuel Witherspoon and Ms. Two Bears?"

"I was cruising the alley behind her place."

"Where was her apartment located?"

"You mean the address?"

"No, I mean what floor? How high up?"

"Second floor."

"Was the window on your squad open or closed when you first heard them?"

"Closed."

"Yet you were able to hear them, in a moving car, with the car window closed, from inside an apartment above you on the second floor, with the door to that apartment nearly closed, am I right?"

"I could've heard them from two blocks away, the way they were going at it."

"So they must have been quite loud?"

"Quite."

"So even though their voices were so loud you could hear them from two blocks away, you did not recognize Samuel Witherspoon's voice, right?"

"I told you, it wasn't just voices. They were throwing stuff around and banging on each other and yelling and screaming. You don't make out individual voices when it's like that."

"What did you do when you heard the voices?"

"I pulled into the alley and parked my unit behind Ms. Two Bears' place, kinda at an angle, partially blocking the alley."

"Why partially blocking the alley?"

"You don't want anyone zipping by taking a shot at you or blocking the alley behind you."

"Is that standard procedure?"

"I dunno. That's the way I do it. I don't know if it's in a book somewhere, but that's the way I learned it."

"Is it standard procedure to call out someone by name?"

"I didn't call him out. He must've heard the unit pull in, because he steps out on the porch."

"Are you aware of Ms. Two Bears' testimony where she said that the victim was called out?"

"Yeah, but she don't know what she's talking about. I didn't call him. He must've heard the car."

"Were your headlights on? Were your flashing lights on?"

"No, I turned them off."

"Why? Wouldn't your lights have illuminated the scene better?"

"Look, he's stepping out on the porch just as I'm pulling in. I see something in his hand. I'm not going to light myself up like a Christmas tree for him to take a potshot at me."

"You say you saw something in his hand. Was the overhead light on the porch on?"

"No."

"You're absolutely sure about that?"

"I'm absolutely sure."

"Because if it had been on, you clearly would have been able to identify Samuel Witherspoon, wouldn't you?"

"Objection. Speculative."

"Your Honor, we can call an expert if we have to, to testify that if a one-hundred-watt GE light bulb had been on directly over Samuel Witherspoon's head, then he would be clearly identifiable from where Defendant was standing when he shot him."

"Ms. Steinmetz, you'll have that opportunity. Sustained."

"So Witherspoon was standing in the dark and you could not identify him, am I correct?"

"Correct."

"Then what happened?"

"Well, as I'm stepping out of the unit, he fires on me. He shoots."

"How many times?"

"Once."

"And what would you estimate the distance from which he fired?"

"Oh, maybe thirty feet as the crow flies."

"He was a trained police officer, trained in the use of firearms, marksmanship, and he misses entirely at a distance of some thirty feet, right?"

"He was a police officer. He sure wasn't at the time. He'd been bounced for psycho. And he was drunk."

"Then what happened?"

"I duck back into the squad, unrack the Ithaca, I kneel behind the door on the driver's side, roll down the window, brace the shotgun on the windowsill on the driver's side, I identify myself, and he fires again, and then I fire, and it's all over. He pitches over the rail. I take a quick look. Most of his head is missing. I go back to the unit, call backup, and they're there in a couple minutes."

"How did you identify yourself?"

"I said, 'Police, put down your weapon.'"

"Do you think he could have misunderstood you? Sometimes 'police' may have sounded like 'please,' couldn't it?"

"Look, the guy was drunk, and I said 'police,' not something else."

"Your Honor, this is the second time Sergeant White has referred to the victim as being drunk. That has not been established. I move to strike."

"Sustained. Jury will disregard Sergeant White's characterization but is free to consider other testimony on this subject that has been admitted."

"And your lights aren't flashing, so he has no way to identify you from your car, does he?" said Steinmetz.

"I believe I already explained that. No, he doesn't."

"Then what happened?"

"Like I said, he takes another shot at me, and I take him down with the shotgun. He goes over, and that's it."

"Why did you go back into your unit for your shotgun? Why didn't you return fire with your handgun after he shot at you the first time?"

"I don't really know. I've thought about that. I mean, I could have saved time and all. I just don't know."

"So the former police officer takes a second shot from about thirty feet, misses again completely, not even hitting the door of your car, and you return fire, and the light breaks, his head is blown off, and he goes over the rail and falls in a snowbank, right?"

"Yeah, that's about right."

"Then what?"

"I called for backup."

"Did you go upstairs, see about Ms. Two Bears?"

"No."

"Do you touch the body?"

"I kinda looked at it, but he was dead. I didn't do nothing else."

"And the gun next to the body was not a throwdown? Am I correct?"

"Yes. No way."

"So I would be absolutely mistaken if I accused you of planting a gun at the scene to make it appear he shot at you, is that correct?"

"That's correct."

"And he did fire at you at least twice, is that correct?"

"Yeah."

"And this is true despite the fact there were no traces of gunpowder or other gun residue on the body when it was examined?"

"Yeah, it's true."

"Did you touch or handle this handgun in any way?"

"No."

"What did you do with your shotgun?"

"I think I was still holding it when Steinmetz got there."

Emily moved on.

Peerless's coaching had not been entirely successful. White was defensive and belligerent when she asked him about the citizen complaints, the $200,000 judgment the city had had to pay to the protester he had injured with his nightstick.

She had gotten what she wanted.

So had Peerless.

Making it clear he felt that she had done nothing to damage his client's credibility, Peerless asked White, "Did you murder Samuel Witherspoon?"

"No, sir."

Peerless casually waved him off the stand.

"The state calls Paul Langseth."

If White was the prototype of the street cop, Langseth was the polar opposite, pudgy, rumpled, balding, bespeckled. He was also a legend in the department as a ballistics expert with an encyclopedic knowledge of handguns.

Emily showed him the handgun found next to Witherspoon, asked him to identify it as the one he had examined, and placed it in evidence.

"Lieutenant Langseth, you've examined the handgun that allegedly was fired by Samuel Witherspoon the night he was killed. Could you summarize your findings for us."

"Sure. It was a nine-inch .22-caliber long-rifle nine-shot Iver Johnson top break double-action revolver."

"Whoa. Let's go over that a bit. I'm not sure we're all as familiar with these terms as you are. First of all, nine inch. What does that mean?"

"The barrel, the part the bullet comes out of, was nine inches long."

"The .22 caliber. What does that mean?"

"It means the handgun fires .22 caliber rounds. The bullets, the lead part, are point 22 millimeters in diameter."

"What does long-rifle mean?"

"It means the type of case or shell, the brass part that holds the bullet. Long-rifle refers to a shell that is a bit longer than a .22 short or a .22 long in order to accommodate a greater amount of gunpowder. It's a common load, used in both handguns and rifles."

"What's a nine-shot?"

"The cylinder, the part that holds the rounds, can hold up to nine rounds."

"I thought revolvers were six-shooters?"

"Well, most are. It's a kind of a quality thing. The more shots, the thinner the separation between the chambers in the cylinder, and the more likely the handgun will heat up and break down. The better revolvers tend to have five or six chambers. Smith and Wesson make some five-shot revolvers, like the Ladysmith."

"The Ladysmith?"

"Yeah, it's what they call a purse gun, a .32, for ladies."

Laughter.

"We're getting quite an education here. Okay, Lieutenant, how about Iver Johnson?"

"Old-time manufacturer. Out of business for a long time now. Used to sell mostly through the big catalog companies."

"So this was not a quality piece?"

"No."

"Was this what they call a Saturday night special?"

"No, too big for that. A plinker. Sometimes they call 'em varmint guns."

"A plinker?"

"For shooting at tin cans, that sort of thing."

"Varmints? What kind of varmints?"

"The idea is, this is sort of a farmer's gun, keep around the barn for chasing off foxes and mice and that sort of thing. I doubt if it really killed many varmints."

"How much would it have retailed for new?"

"It so happens I brought a Monkey Ward catalogue with me."

"Your Honor, we'll ask that this be marked and entered into evidence as state's exhibit number, let's see, 22."

"Objections? Okay, mark it please as state's 22. Received."

"Okay, Lieutenant Langseth. What's the date of the catalog?"

"It's 1956."

"What's the price of the revolver?"

"That's $29.95, plus shipping."

"Pretty cheap?"

"Yeah."

"Anybody could buy one?"

"In those days, just about."

"How many do you suppose in circulation?"

"Objection. Speculative."

"Your Honor, may I rephrase?"

"Yes."

"Do you know how many were manufactured and sold?"

"Yeah." He pulled out a piece of paper from his coat jacket. "It's 347,827 from 1928 until 1963, when the model was discontinued."

"What are you reading from?"

"United States Bureau of Alcohol, Tobacco, and Firearms firearms figures."

"State wishes to place this in evidence as state's exhibit number twenty-three."

"No objections. Received. Please mark it as state's number twenty-three."

"Lieutenant, what's the serial number on this particular handgun."

"Y0786561-411."

"Can you determine from the serial number when this was manufactured?"

"Yes, 1934, according to those federal reports I gave you."

"That's 1934, thirty years before Samuel Witherspoon was even born."

"Objection. Counsel is testifying again."

"Sustained. Jury will disregard."

"Okay, now, Lieutenant, explain top break, please."

"It means that the cylinder does not swing out from the frame like in most revolvers. You push a release with your right thumb, and the gun opens up at the top, the barrel tilts downward, exposing the cylinder. There's a little spring under the cylinder, so it kind of pops up, and the cartridges kind of pop out."

"What's the purpose of this design?"

"Quick load. In some revolvers, single-actions mostly, there's a little gate on the side and a spring-operated rod so you can push out the rounds, but you have to unload one chamber at a time."

"Is the top-break feature kind of unusual, like the nine-shot feature?"

"Yeah. Iver Johnson were the only ones who manufactured it, and then only in the .22."

"Why was that?"

"Well, because it's inherently unstable. Instead of being a solid one-piece frame, the barrel and the frame were separate. This is a gun that tends to spit lead."

"What's that?"

"Because they're separate, the cylinder and the barrel don't always align properly, and it doesn't help when you got nine shots and much less margin for error between the chambers, so when it's fired, pieces of the bullet tend to shear off instead of going through the barrel. The Iver Johnson people knew it too, that's why they only made it in a .22, but even a .22 releases a hell of a lot of energy."

"Would a handgun that spits lead also tend to release an inordinate amount of gunpowder residue?"

"Objection. Vague. What is inordinate? It's purely subjective."

"Sustained. Rephrase, Counsel."

"Lieutenant, in your expert opinion, does the design of the Iver Johnson nine-shot top break .22 double action revolver tend to result in causing the firing of the gun to release amounts of lead and gunpowder residue in excess of the amounts in most other handguns with which you are familiar?"

"Yes."

"Okay, now what about double-action?"

"Means you can fire just by pulling the trigger. With a single-action, you have to cock it by pulling the hammer back before you can fire."

"What's revolver mean?"

"It means that as you pull the trigger, the cylinder revolves."

"What happens when you pull the trigger on a double-action revolver?"

"The trigger mechanism engages the hammer, which is on a spring. The hammer goes back until it passes a release point, where it disengages from the trigger mechanism, and the spring then propels it back to the frame. As this is happening, the cylinder revolves, placing a fresh cartridge directly under the hammer. The firing pin mounted on the head of the hammer strikes the end of the cartridge. This causes the gunpowder inside the cartridge to ignite, converting it from a solid to a powerful gas which forces the bullet out the barrel."

"What you've just described is standard operating procedure, right?"

"Right."

"But as you've pointed out, this particular handgun is unusual in several respects, am I right?"

"Yes."

"In what respects other than those you have already described?"

"The cylinder rotates counterclockwise. In every other handgun I'm aware of, the cylinder rotates clockwise."

"Does that affect your findings with respect to the handgun which was allegedly fired at Defendant by Samuel Witherspoon on the night Witherspoon was killed?"

"Yes."

"Were you in the courtroom when defendant testified about being shot at by the victim?"

"Yes."

"Did you hear Defendant say he was fired at twice by Witherspoon?"

"Objection. Leading."

"Sustained. Rephrase."

"What did you hear Defendant say with respect to being fired upon by the victim?"

"That the victim fired at him at least twice."

"Do your examination of the handgun found beside Samuel Witherspoon's body support the defendant's statement that the victim fired on him at least twice?"

"No."

"Why?"

"Because in this handgun, the cylinder rotated counterclockwise, so that if there were two rounds in the piece and two rounds were fired, and nobody messed with the gun after it was recovered, so the first round would have moved to the left of the hammer when the second one was fired, and the second one would stay under the hammer. White testified Witherspoon fired on him twice before he got off. If that's true, there should have been one spent round on the left side of the hammer, one under the hammer. There wasn't. There was a spent round under the hammer and a spent round on the right. That's the usual pattern, but it's not right for this piece."

"So in your expert opinion, what do you conclude about the firing of this handgun on the night of Samuel Witherspoon's death?"

"It wasn't fired the way White testified. It was a throwdown."

"Thank you. Your witness."

Peerless went over to the exhibit table.

"Your Honor, if I may, I would like to examine this handgun, but to tell you the truth, these things make me kind of nervous. Could we ask the bailiff to make sure it isn't loaded?"

"Certainly." The bailiff checked it out and handed the piece to Peerless, who held it pointing downward with his finger outside the trigger guard.

"Lieutenant, if I recall correctly, you testified that the gun couldn't have been fired the way Sergeant White described in his testimony because of the position of the cylinder, am I correct?"

"Yes. I said that, assuming the gun was not tampered with after it was recovered."

"Ah, not tampered with. You also, I believe, testified that you heard Sergeant White's testimony with respect to the firing of the gun, am I right?"

"Yes."

"Then you heard him testify that a total of two shots were fired at him, right?"

"Right."

"Is it possible that someone who fired two shots at Sergeant White could also have wanted to fire three shots at him?"

"Yes."

"In fact, it's possible isn't it, based on the testimony you heard, that Mr. Witherspoon was in the process of trying to shoot Sergeant White for the third time, when he himself was shot?"

"It's possible."

"Lieutenant, you say this is a double-action piece, am I right?"

"Yes."

"Now, if I'm not mistaken, a double-action piece can also be fired single-action, can it not?"

"Yes."

"And when you fire single-action, you pull back the hammer with your thumb, and then you pull the trigger?"

"Doesn't have to be with your thumb, but that's the usual way if you're going to fire single-action," said Langseth.

"And in the process of pulling back the trigger with your thumb, you hear a kind of click, click, click as you go through various, shall we say, stages of engagement between the hammer and cylinder, is that correct?"

"Yes."

"And on the second click, the cylinder freewheels, doesn't it?"

"Yes."

"So Samuel Witherspoon could have been pulling back the hammer and got as far as the second click, getting ready to take that third shot at that very instant when he was hit, right?"

"It's possible."

"And then he loses control of the gun. And it falls out of his hand. And then..." said Peerless. He pulled back the trigger two clicks with his right thumb. Then, with his left hand, he spun the cylinder, which rotated freely for several seconds and then stopped.

"Round and round she goes, and where she stops, nobody knows," said Peerless. He didn't wait for an answer.

"Thank you. Lieutenant, that will be all."

CHAPTER 13

It had been a long day for Emily. It got longer when the mayor called her into his office. Reagan was already there.

"Not going too well, is it?" said Sensaboe.

"We're not done yet," said Reagan.

"And the cops are still out there," said Sensaboe.

"They're about the same number as before, maybe a few less," said Reagan.

"Or maybe a few more," said Sensaboe. "Did you see the signs? 'Reagan and Sensaboe: Crime fighters or cop haters?'"

"Okay, look," said Reagan. "The sun shines on every dog's ass. There's more. Donovan's tomorrow."

"Good," said Sensaboe. "I'm counting on you." Emily hadn't spoken.

"Thanks, Chief," she said after they left. "Is this what cops mean when they talk about having a rabbi?"

"Emily, you're doing all the heavy lifting," said Reagan. "I'm just trying to keep Hizzoner from losing his nerve."

*****

Detective Inspector Raymond M. Donovan was a practiced witness who had testified in hundreds of criminal trials. Emily wasted no time in getting to the point.

"Did you conduct an examination of the scene?"

"Yes."

"And in the course of that examination, did you examine the light fixture on the porch where the victim was standing at the time he was killed?"

"Yes."

"And were you present when Defendant White testified as to the whether the porch light was on or off at the time he discharged his shotgun?"

"Yes."

"And do you recall his testimony?"

"Yes."

"And how do you recall how he testified as to whether the porch light was on or off at the time he fired his shotgun?"

"Yes. He said the light was off."

"Do you recall whether he was asked if he was certain that the porch light was off?"

"Yes."

"Do you recall how he answered?"

"Yes."

"How did he answer?"

"He said 'absolutely.'"

"He was absolutely certain the porch light was off?"

"Yes."

"Based on your examination of the porch light, could you determine whether the porch light was in fact off when the shot was fired?"

"Yes, I could make a determination."

"How were you able to make that determination?"

"By examining the filament of the light bulb in the light fixture."

"Did you make that examination?"

"Yes."

"When?"

"When I arrived at the scene."

"When was that?"

"About forty-five minutes after the incident."

"Had anyone else examined the fixture prior to that time?"

"Not that I'm aware of. The only person who had been on the porch was Lieutenant Steinmetz when he went to talk with Gloria Two Bears."

"How did your examination enable you to make a determination whether the porch light was on or off when Samuel Witherspoon was shot?"

"Because when a light bulb is broken while the light is turned on, the filament turns black. That's because the gas in the light bulb is heated, which causes the gas to react to the oxygen in the atmosphere and burn rapidly and carbonize the metal in the filament, turning it black. When a light bulb is off when the bulb is broken, the metal in the filament, at most, turns a light gray because the gas in the light bulb is cool and dissipates into the atmosphere without reacting to the oxygen."

"Based on what you have just testified to as to the chemical reactions that take place in broken light bulbs, could you tell us whether the porch light was on or off when it was broken?"

"Yes."

"Was it off or on?"

"It was on."

"How did you determine that?"

"The filament was black and curled up. It had burned up. The light was on when Witherspoon was shot."

There was a buzz in the courtroom. Gunderson gavelled vigorously.

"Did you subsequently conduct another examination of the scene?"

"Yes."

"What was the purpose of that examination?"

"To determine if someone walking or standing on the porch under the light with the light on would be identifiable to someone standing in the alley."

"When was this examination conducted?"

"Actually, we did it twice. Two weeks after the shooting at one a.m. in the morning, same weather conditions, and then again two nights after the first time."

"How did you conduct that examination?"

"We had an officer walk back and forth under the light and also stand under the light."

"What were the results of your examination?"

"The person would be clearly identifiable."

"What do you mean 'clearly identifiable'?"

"That you could easily determine who it was that was on the porch if you were in the alley where Sergeant White said he was standing."

"Thank you. Your witness."

Eddie White had turned to stone, but Peerless never changed expressions. Chipping away at the tiny openings, he managed to get Donovan to admit that it was possible that if Witherspoon had turned off the light when he stepped out onto the porch and the shots had been exchanged immediately afterward that the gases in the bulb might not have had time to cool completely, and the burned filament might have been "darker than light gray." And while Peerless wasn't exactly playing the race card, he got Donovan to admit that, yes, black folks might be a little harder to identify in the dark under one-hundred-watt light than white folks.

"Your witness, Ms. Steinmetz."

"Detective Inspector Donovan, where was the switch for the porch light located?" said Emily.

"At the head of the stairs."

"So that someone leaving Ms. Two Bears' apartment would have had to pass under the light to get from the apartment to the light switch to turn it off, is that correct?"

"Yes."

"And then, if they were to be showered by fragments from the light bulb, they would have had to be under the light, wouldn't they?"

"Yes."

"Detective Inspector Donovan, who was on the porch when you were conducting your subsequent examinations as to whether someone was identifiable under the light?"

"Officer Curtis Spears."

"What race is Officer Spears?"

"African American."

"Thank you. Your witness."

Peerless gave it another go.

"If someone were to leave Ms. Two Bears' apartment and walk across the porch to turn off the light switch, how long would they be under that light?"

"A couple of seconds."

"Even less than that, wouldn't you say?"

"No, because they would be visible the entire time they were walking across the porch. That's the whole idea behind a porch light, so you can see where you're going in the dark."

"And are you claiming that at one a.m. in the morning, an African American male, crossing under a one-hundred-watt light bulb for a second would be identifiable to someone he hadn't seen for years standing in an alley thirty feet away?"

"To a trained police officer, yes."

"How about to a trained police officer pulling an 8:00 p.m. to 4:00 a.m. shift for the third night in a row, maybe a little tired, maybe not quite as attentive as he should be?"

"Sergeant White should have been able to identify Witherspoon under those circumstances. We try not to send out people when they're exhausted or overstressed."

"Try not to?"

"That's right."

"Thank you. No further questions."

"Ms. Steinmetz?"

"Just one, Your Honor. Detective Inspector Donovan, isn't it fact that Sergeant White was sufficiently alert to avoid two bullets, if there were in fact two bullets, and to take down Witherspoon with a head shot?"

"Objection. Leading. Argumentative. Move to strike."

"Sustained. Jury will disregard. Ms. Steinmetz?"

"I have nothing further, Your Honor."

"All right, witness, that will be all. You may step down. Ms. Steinmetz, do you have any further witnesses before the state rests?"

"Yes, Your Honor, just one. The state calls Ramona Guiterrez."

CHAPTER 14

Ramona Guiterrez had phoned Donovan the day before and told him she had decided to come back and would testify. He asked her what she planned to say, but she refused to tell him.

When Emily called her at her hotel, Ramona agreed to meet with her in her suite that evening.

Emily would have preferred they meet at her office, but she was too exhausted to argue. Anyway, it was probably a good idea to meet away from the courthouse, the House of Whispers being an accurate description of the place.

"Senora Guiterrez, I'm pleased to meet you," Emily said, trying to see her with first impression eyes and gauge how a jury would react to her. Not bad, she thought. A little too much makeup, a little too much of the Great Lady about her, but a certain vulnerability behind the facade.

"Thank you for coming," Guiterrez said.

The coffee first. Then the weather. Then the changes to Sanasauk since Guiterrez had left. Not many really. Then they got down to business.

"You came a long way, Senora Guiterrez. What can you tell us?"

"I can tell you about Samuel. I knew him. Quite well."

"Yes, that will be helpful. Can you tell us why he was killed?"

"Yes."

"Why?"

"Because they were afraid he would talk."

"About what?"

"I wish to testify."

"I know that. But I must know what you wish to testify to."

"I was in the courtroom yesterday. Sitting in the back. I was the one in the dark glasses. You looked over at me a couple of times. I thought perhaps you knew who I was. You are losing this case. The jury will not convict this man. I will tell them why Samuel was killed. That is what I will testify to. That is all you need to know."

"Senora Guiterrez, I must know what you are going to say."

"No, I will say what I have to say when you call me to testify. And you will call me. You have no choice. We both know that. Thank you for coming. Good night."

*****

When Ramona Guiterrez took the stand the next day, the excess makeup was gone. Watching her, Donovan remembered that she had arranged their meeting at the Hippodrome so she always would be seated. Now he realized why. She had a slight, almost imperceptible limp, more of an imbalance really, as though one side were slightly stronger than the other. It could be just a pelvic tilt, but he thought it was probably the result of childhood polio. Perhaps her parents had not believed in immunization. He had heard somewhere that some first-generation Chicanos were suspicious of Anglo medicine. He wondered how she had managed to hide it when she took her departmental physical. Younger then, less heavy, not so tired or worn as she was today. "Senora Guiterrez, how did you happen to know the victim, Samuel Witherspoon?"

"We served together on the Sanasauk Police Department. We were partners."

"Is that all?"

"No. We were lovers too."

"Did your relationship continue after you left the department?"

"Yes."

"When was the last time you saw Samuel Witherspoon?"

"Three months before he was killed."

"Where was that?"

"In Lexington, Kentucky. I was there for the fall yearling auction. My husband had to leave early to return to Mexico City for some business thing that came up. I called Samuel, and he drove down. It's only a couple hours' drive."

"How long did you stay together?"

"Two nights."

"What happened when he got there?"

"I hadn't seen him for about a year. He didn't look too good. He had gained a lot of weight. He was having trouble making a living since they had made him leave the police force."

"What was he doing for a living?"

"They had gotten him some bouncer jobs, that sort of thing."

"Who is they?"

"The Federation. Eddie White."

"Did he say why Defendant was getting him jobs?"

"Yes. He said Eddie told him that he liked him and wanted to help him, but he thought Eddie wanted to keep an eye on him too."

"Why?"

"Because he knew about killing those two black boys in the cornfield."

"Objection," said Peerless. "This is irrelevant and highly inflammatory and hearsay. The victim is not here to testify as to what he said."

"Your Honor, this is a question of the victim's state of mind, not his veracity. It bears on the motive for the crime here. This whole matter is about a continuing event that began in that cornfield."

"The objection is overruled. This incident appears to be connected to the actions we are considering here. Continue, Ms. Steinmetz."

"Senora Guiterrez, are you saying Mr. Witherspoon was frightened?"

"Objection. She's leading the witness."

"Sustained. Jury will disregard."

"Senora Guiterrez, were you able to determine the victim's state of mind?"

"Yes. He was afraid."

"And why was he afraid of Defendant?"

"Defendant? No, he liked Eddie, but Eddie was just a tool of the other one. He was afraid of your ex-husband, Ms. Lady Lawyer. Steinmetz. That was the one he was afraid of."

"Why?"

The instant Emily asked, she realized she had made a mistake. She had always sensed there was more, much more, to those killings than he had told her, but she had denied herself the right to pursue it. She had married him. She owed him that much. Yet in her heart's heart, she knew what he had done. She knew why she had asked, and she knew what the answer would be. She had always known.

"Because he killed those colored boys in the cornfield."

The courtroom erupted. Gunderson gavelled away like he was pounding the Golden Spike for the Union Pacific. It finally quieted down.

"The official departmental investigation—in which you gave testimony, under oath—states that Sergeant White shot them in a gunfight."

"Yes, I know. I lied. I was afraid of Lieutenant Steinmetz then. I am afraid of him now. But I cannot be afraid my whole life. I cannot hide away forever. I was there. Sergeant White didn't even get there until after Lieutenant Steinmetz had shot them. Samuel got there first. He was going to arrest them and bring them in. They were running away. Samuel caught up with them and made them stop. Then Lieutenant Steinmetz, he gets there. The boys are standing there, very frightened, and Lieutenant Steinmetz, he's very drunk, and he says to them, 'Get down on your knees, niggers, because even though you're going to hell, you don't want to die without saying your prayers, which is more than you gave Dave Hope,' and then he shoots them, and by that time Sergeant White is there, and Steinmetz, he gives the gun to Sergeant White—Officer White—and he says, 'You're the man, Eddie, you did it, you can make sergeant on this. You turn in the gun. I can't.' So White takes the gun and gives him his gun. Later, Samuel tells me Steinmetz had seen his old girlfriend that night with another man, the guy who got tossed out of a window a couple of years later, and that's why he got drunk."

"You said the boys didn't have firearms?"

"I didn't say, but no, they didn't have guns. Steinmetz had throwdowns. He always carried them. He always carried light bulbs in his glove compartment too. He bragged to Samuel that once he was about to arrest a burglar when the burglar called him a filthy name, and then he shot him in the knee and switched light bulbs and said he shot him in a gunfight in the dark."

"Senora Guiterrez, are you trying to make us believe that Lieutenant Steinmetz set up Sergeant White so that he would kill Samuel Witherspoon and make it look like murder?"

"Why not? Two birds with one stone."

"So after lying under oath at the time of the original investigation, now after—"

"Objection, Counsel is impeaching her own witness."

"Sidebar, please, Your Honor," said Emily.

"Granted."

"Your Honor," said Emily, "yesterday, when I first heard this witness had come here and was willing to testify, I tried to get her to give me an idea what she was going to say, but she refused to tell me. It's now clear she is hostile to the state's case, and I ask permission to cross-examine her under the rules. If I am not allowed to do that, Mr. Jackson here will simply waive his right to cross-examination, and we will never have the opportunity to test Senora Guiterrez's testimony."

"Your Honor, I have an obligation to protect my client's interests here. I can't be required to challenge a witness who appears to be supportive of my client's innocence."

"Ms. Steinmetz, in the interest of justice and of getting to the bottom of this matter, I will permit you to treat Senora Guiterrez as a hostile witness and cross-examine her under the rules.

"Your objection is overruled, Mr. Jackson. Continue."

"Senora Guiterrez, you admit you lied under oath to the departmental investigators when they originally investigated this matter. Why should we believe you now?"

"Because…because someone told me once, there is a God, and he waits and waits for us to do the right thing."

CHAPTER 15

Three weeks later. Mayor Sensaboe's office.

"You know it's a funny thing about these river towns, Chief," said Sensaboe. "They start at the river, then turn their backs on it for the next hundred years, and then they realize it's the greatest asset they've got, and they go back to the river. That's the big fight I got now, get the junk yards and scrap dealers out and put the jogging trails and the high-rises and the piers in."

"Another funny thing is that they never put their city halls down by the river. Know why that is?" said Reagan.

"No," said Sensaboe.

"Well, neither do I, not for sure, anyway, but I think it's because there's always a jail in city halls, to make it easy on the cops to run these guys up to the courtrooms, and they didn't want it too close to the river because if they ever busted out, it would be harder to track them than it would be in the center of town."

"Really?"

"Why else would the politicians accept a less desirable location for their offices? But as I say, I'm not sure."

"You're not sure? Polymaths are always sure, but they're not always right. You were right about the strike, though. They finally took the three percent. They never should have tied their wagons to those two bozos."

"And the jury was right to acquit White. Steinmetz tried to set him up, switching the broken light bulbs and gaffing the throwdown to try and make a liar out of White," said Reagan. "Though Peerless handled the gun thing beautifully. The cylinder *could* have spun around and made it only *appear* to be a throwdown. It was Steinmetz who made the phone call from The Lodge. He knew Witherspoon hung there. Probably tells Olson to check the license plates in the parking lot while he runs in to take a leak or something. 'Eddie, there's a big drug dealer heading out the door with Gloria, you can be a hero again, this time make lute.'"

"I agree with you he made the phone call, Chief, but I think Eddie White knew exactly who he was taking down."

"The light was off. He couldn't tell it was Witherspoon," said Reagan.

"Unless Steinmetz told him when he called."

"Well, we'll never know that, will we?"

"No."

"Most of them eat their guns. But I suppose if you go into a bridge abutment at 80 mph with a skinful of Cutty Sark, there's always that lingering doubt it could have been an accident," said Reagan.

"It's a hard way to go."

"Lieutenant. Locum tenens. You know what that means?"

"No."

"The man who holds the place. That's what Steinmetz was supposed to have done out in the cornfield. That's why we promoted him to lieutenant, because he was supposed to be the one to hold the place," said Reagan.

"You know, I wonder why you didn't get rid of the guy a long time ago."

"I had my suspicions, but I was never able to confirm them."

"Oh? That's not what the boys at the pistol range told me."

"What did they tell you?"

"They told me you made a call out there. It was a long time ago, but it was such an unusual request they made a record of it. After this whole White-Steinmetz thing came down, they decided to remember it, and one of them stopped by to see me. It seems you had them record the serial number on Steinmetz's handgun. Turns out it was the same as the serial number Eddie White registered with the department as his official piece. You must have had a pretty good idea by that time what happened out at the cornfield. Why didn't you do something then?"

"Let's just say Lieutenant Steinmetz and I had an understanding."

"You mean you both had things you would rather not have bandied about in public?"

"You could say that."

"Chief, do you recall when we first talked about your coming to Sanasauk?"

"Sure."

"You told me you were concerned about fitting in here with all us stoic Northern European types? That reminds me of when I was a teenager. I thought I wanted to be a stock trader. My dad was a lawyer, and he'd given me a few shares of a local company for my birthday, and I held it for a while, and then I sold it at a profit, and then I decided it was going to go down, so I sold it short, and I made money on that too," said Sensaboe.

"There's nothing like making money on a short. The rush is like a big gambling score. There's a line I love from *The Color of Money*: 'Money won is sweeter than money earned,'" said Reagan.

"My dad saw where that was heading," said Sensaboe.

"There's nothing worse than beginner's luck for turning a dumb kid into a degenerate gambler for life, so he took me down to Chicago, the big options exchange, all those traders standing around the big action posts—in those days it was IBM and Xerox—yelling and screaming at each other.

"'What do see there, son?' he said.

"'I see a lot of guys standing around yelling and screaming at each other. Looks exciting,' I said.

"'It is. But that isn't what I see. I see a lot of Jews, Irishmen, and Italians standing around yelling and screaming at each other, but I don't see any Sensaboes. No Swedes. No Norwegians. No Krauts,' he said.

"I decided he was right. So I went to law school, got turned on to civil rights, spent my summers in Mississippi registering voters because I thought that was the way I could make a difference, and wound up here.

"I turn on CNBC sometimes when I get up in the morning, just to see how the market's doing, and there they are: Faber and Kieran and Bartiroma, and then there's Greenberg and McCulloch and Pisano, ad infinitum, and there still aren't any Sensaboes. There's things we're good at, and there's things they're good at. There's places we belong, and there's places they belong.

"You were right about Sanasauk, Chief. Did I ever tell you the story about Billy Martin and the two envelopes?"

About the Author

Dan Cohen is the author of a recent crime novel, City of Stones, in collaboration with Christopher Valen. He also wrote Undefeated: A Biography of Hubert Humphrey and Anonymous Source: At War with the Media, the story of his successful United States Supreme Court case, Cohen v. Cowles Media 501 US 663 (1991) in which the press was found liable for having broken their promise to treat Cohen as an anonymous source when Cohen provided truthful information that a candidate for statewide office was a convicted shoplifter. Cohen also wrote a dozen children's mini mysteries and a collection of short stories, Habitual Offenders, and ghosted five business self-help books and wrote the History of Breck School: A Journey. He is a graduate of Stanford University and Harvard Law School and has been admitted to the Minnesota Bar. He is a former president of the Minneapolis City Council and former president of the Minneapolis Planning Commission. He also previously served as a member of the Minneapolis Charter Commission. Honorable Discharge, US Navy (US Naval Reserve 1954–1962).